# *BLUESDAY*

Adrienne Thompson

Pink Cashmere Publishing Company

USA

Edited by Alyndria Mooney

Cover Design by Corey A. Burkes

This is a work of fiction. Names, characters, businesses,
places, events and incidents are either the products of the
author's imagination or used in a fictitious manner. Any
resemblance to actual persons, living or dead, or actual
events is purely coincidental.

Printed in the United States of America

First Printing 2011

ISBN: 0983756902
ISBN-13: 978-0-9837569-0-3

*To God be the glory! We did it, Lord!*


*This book is dedicated to the places and people of my childhood. May the spirit of love and community that is found in Willisville, Arkansas bless all who read this.*


*To Aunt Velma, Uncle Zeke, and Aunt Jarva. I miss you.
To Mama and Aunt Jean, I love you.*

*And most of all be warm in your love for one another;*
*because in love there is forgiveness for sins without number.*

*1 Peter 4:8*

## Soundtrack

"The Blues Is Alright" *Little Milton*
"Blues Before Sunrise" *John Lee Hooker*
"I'm Tore Down" *Freddie King*
"Ain't No Love in the Heart of the City" *Bobby "Blue" Bland*
"Members Only" *Bobby "Blue" Bland*
"St. James Infirmary" *Bobby "Blue" Bland*
"Down Home Blues" *Z.Z. Hill*
"Sweet Sixteen" *B.B. King*
"Preaching the Blues" *Son House*
"Spoonful" *Howlin' Wolf*
"Still Called the Blues" *Johnnie Taylor*
"The Truth Will Set You Free" *The Revelations feat. Tre' Williams*
"You Can't Lose What You Ain't Never Had" *Muddy Waters*
"Someday After While" *Freddie King*
"Still Crazy For You" *Johnnie Taylor*
"That's Alright" *John Lee Hooker*
"Please Accept My Love" *B.B. King*
"You've Got to Hurt Before You Heal" *Bobbie "Blue" Bland*
"Cheaper to Keep Her" *Johnnie Taylor*
"Blues Power" *Albert King*
"Confessing the Blues" *Little Walter*
"Baby, Please Don't Go" *Big Joe Williams*
"Waiting For Your Call" *B.B. King*
"Sky is Crying" *Albert King*
"Ain't Understanding Mellow?" *Jerry Butler and Brenda Lee Eager*

# Part One

# Intro

# ONE

### "The Blues Is Alright"

"LADIES and gentlemen, without further ado, I present to you the 'Baby Girl of Blues'. The one and only Ms. Bobbie BluAnn Brooks!" The announcer's enthusiastic proclamation elated the near-capacity crowd inside of the House of Blues. They erupted into cheers and applause as the band began playing "Messed Up," one of her biggest hits. She strutted onstage with a small, clear plastic cup in one hand which, upon closer inspection, would reveal itself to be half full of an unequal mixture of whisky and coke, boasting a majority of whisky. With the other hand she grabbed the microphone from its stand and with brick red-painted lips began belting out the lyrics:

> *"Well I think I'm 'bout to lose my man.*
> *You see he just don't understand.*
> *I love the way he makes me feel.*
> *But listen up, here's the deal*

*I got this fine brother on the side*
*And I love the way he makes me shine*
*I really wanna leave him alone*
*Don't wanna mess up my happy home*

*But his lovin's so good*
*It's a crying shame*
*I can't make up my mind*
*And he's to blame*
*You see on one hand I got a man who loves me*
*And on the other hand, I got a man who sho' nuff rubs me*

*So I'm stuck, messed up*
*Sick and stressed out*
*But I can't stop what I'm doing*
*And baby's putting me out…"*

The bright spotlight illuminated her every move. Bobbie quickly captivated the audience as she batted her eyelashes, rocked her hips to the music, and raised her arms in the air. She wore extra tight, black leather leggings, a black pair of dominatrix-style six-inch heels, and a white designer tank top. Around her neck hung a silver chain and suspended from it, a huge diamond cross. Her unruly afro of soft, messy curls shook as she bobbed her head to the music. Bobbie possessed hard-core rock and roll style, but her sound was undeniably down-home blues. She had often been described as a young Etta James and being compared to one of the greats was quite an honor for Bobbie.

Named after her father's favorite blues artist, Bobbie "Blue" Bland, she was at the top of her game. Bobbie began performing professionally at the age of eighteen and was entering her twelfth year as a rather successful blues artist, frequenting blues venues and festivals throughout the country. This performance in Chicago was one of the many stops on her tour to promote her latest CD, *Bluesday*.

She was a beautiful woman, standing 5'2" and 150 pounds with full soft curves, almond-shaped black-brown eyes, pouty lips, and honey brown skin. She was so sexy that all of the men wanted her and so sassy that all of the women wanted to *be* her.

Bobbie finished the opening song and placed the mic back in its stand. She grabbed a black towel off of a stool sitting on the stage and wiped the sweat from her brow, then took a sip of her drink.

She took the mic from its stand, smiled, and with a southern drawl she said, "How y'all doing out there?"

The crowd roared in response.

Bobbie took another swig of her drink. "Y'all better be feeling *great*. Got me up here sweating off my make-up already!"

The crowd roared again and a man yelled, "We love you, Bobbie!" from within the crowd.

Bobbie winked at the audience and smiled seductively. "I love you too, baby! Come on y'all, let's get *down*! Woo! Here we go!"

With that, she continued through her usual set of songs. To them she'd added two songs from *Bluesday*, "My Fault" and "Just Right". She closed the show as she always did with her rendition of "Members Only", a Bobby "Blue" Bland classic. This was how she'd ended all of her performances ever since she was a youngster, singing in small Arkansas jukes. Her finale always brought the house down.

When the show was over, Bobbie took her final bow, and shouted, "Thank you Chi-Town! Y'all were great!" into the microphone before strutting off the stage with the remnants of her drink in her hand. She left the spotlight behind and walked through the darkness into her small dressing room.

Waiting in her dressing room was Clyde Morgan, Bobbie's manager and her husband of six years. The small space was filled with the scent of his favorite cologne. Polo.

"You were wonderful, little girl," he said, slipping his cell phone into the pocket of his olive green slacks. He stood up from a folding chair and kissed Bobbie on the cheek. "But then again, you always are."

Bobbie tilted her face towards him and smiled. "Thank you, baby. Who were you talking to on the phone?"

He shrugged. "Oh nobody, baby. Just working out some deals for you. You know I'm always working hard for you, girl."

Bobbie pursed her lips. "Mm hmm."

She had long believed that Clyde was cheating on her but had never been able to find any concrete proof. Besides, she was crazy about him. Bobbie idolized and adored her father and in some ways one could say that Clyde was his replacement, although he looked nothing like her father. While Bobbie's father, Earl Brooks, was a tall thin medium brown-skinned man with deep-set, dark eyes; Clyde was a compact 5'6". He was pale brown-skinned with clear, gray eyes and sandy-colored hair.

She'd married Clyde shortly after her father had passed away, when she was only twenty-four years old. He was twenty years her senior and had been her manager for her entire professional career.

It was Clyde who'd negotiated her first record deal and he'd been overseeing every aspect of her career and life ever since. It was an arrangement that seemed to suit both Clyde and Bobbie well.

"Well, I guess you know Sabrina got sick again tonight and couldn't perform. I'm really getting tired of her, Clyde. You need to hire me a new back-up singer and get rid of her tail," Bobbie said as she began to undress.

"Aw, baby. The girl can't help it if she's sickly. Cut her some slack."

"Clyde, I been cutting her *too* much slack. Every other show she's got some problem that keeps her from going on. I'm tired of her. She's just unreliable and unprofessional. I mean, how many times have I gone on even when I didn't feel like it?"

Clyde stepped behind Bobbie and began to rub her bare shoulders. "That's what makes *you* the star, little girl. Look, we'll talk about hiring someone else after the tour is over, okay?" He purred the words into Bobbie's ear and then kissed her neck.

She melted against his body and relented. "Well, alright then."

"Go on, baby," he said, patting her on her ample behind. "Get ready for the after-party. I'll be in the car waiting for you."

Bobbie smiled. "Okay. I'll be ready in a little bit."

Bobbie sat down at the make-up table and freshened-up as she finished off her drink. Bobbie always did her own hair and make-up because Clyde had wanted it that way. His motto was, "Why pay someone else to do what you can do for yourself for free?" Bobbie chose her own wardrobe as well, no stylist. For the after-party, she changed into a form-fitting red strapless dress that stopped midway her thighs. The dress clung to her wide hips and revealed enough cleavage to catch the attention of any man within a ten-mile radius. As she searched through a suitcase for matching shoes, she popped open a bottle of Champaign someone had sent her, Moët and Chandon. She poured some into her cup and as she sipped it, found a pair of thigh-high black leather boots. She picked her hair out with her finger tips, replaced her brick red lipstick with a shade of true red, and then stumbled out of the dressing room, Champaign bottle and trusty cup in hand.

Outside, she stepped into the cool Chicago evening air and then into Clyde's rented Cadillac STS as he waited for her behind the wheel.

Clyde shook his head in disgust as she climbed into the car. "You gotta have a drink with you everywhere you go, Bobbie?"

Bobbie held her hand up and looked at Clyde. "Look, don't start that tonight. Let's just go, Clyde," she slurred.

Clyde put the car in gear and began to pull off the lot. "Bobbie, you gonna turn into an alcoholic if you don't watch it. You're gonna ruin your career and mess up everything we built."

She laughed as she settled into the beige leather seat. "*We* built? Whatever Clyde, just hush up and drive."

Clyde stopped the car at the edge of the lot and looked at her. He raised his eyebrows and brought his face closer to hers. "Watch your mouth, little girl. I ain't your chauffer. I *made* you and don't think I can't break you."

Bobbie rolled her eyes. "Really, Mr. Morgan? Last I checked, Mae and Earl Brooks *made* me. I don't think you were present for the occasion."

Clyde's facial expression hardened and his eyes darkened. He reached over and tightly grasped Bobbie's wrist. She tried to jerk away but was no match for his strength.

"I'mma say this one more time, little girl. WATCH YOUR MOUTH! You don't want none of this tonight, *believe me*." He released her and began to pull off of the lot.

Bobbie turned and looked out the window without saying another word.

Clyde shook his head and added, "See, that's what I'm talking about right there. You get all that liquor in you and you lose your damn mind. It makes you think you can talk to me any kinda way when you know better. You know I don't take that kinda mess from *no one*."

Bobbie kept her eyes on the scenery outside of her window,

knowing that another word from her would only escalate things with Clyde. They rode in silence the remainder of the ride to the night club where the party was being held, but once they'd arrived, she plastered on a happy face and worked the party like the star she was, smiling and talking to everyone she saw as she mingled through the crowd. Drunk or not, she was always the consummate performer, whether on or off-stage. She hugged well-wishers and graciously thanked those who congratulated her on a successful show. Bobbie had a way of making everyone feel like they were in her inside track. They never knew if she didn't recognize them or remember meeting them before. She made everyone feel like they were an important part of her life.

Clyde, as usual, disappeared from sight several times throughout the evening. When she was able to locate him, he'd either be in a dark corner on his cell phone or claim to have been in the restroom.

"This beer is running right through me," he'd say, although Bobbie hadn't seen him with a single solitary drink all night.

As the party wound down and the club began to empty, an exhausted Bobbie found that Clyde had once again disappeared. After waiting for an hour, a droopy-eyed Bobbie finally took a cab back to the Blackstone Hotel.

Once she'd arrived at her room, she dug the key card out of her small purse and opened the door to find that Clyde was not there either. After showering and dressing for bed, she tried to call Clyde's cell. It rang straight to voice mail. She tried to wait up for him but ended up drifting off to sleep on the sofa, with her cell phone in her hand.

# TWO

### "Blues Before Sunrise"

A knock at the door jarred Bobbie from a sound sleep. She checked the time on her cell phone through squinted eyes and saw that it was ten in the morning. She sat there for a few more moments, stiff from having slept on the sofa, and then realized that maybe it was Clyde knocking at the door. *Maybe he lost his key,* she thought. She stumbled to her feet, stretched, and wrapped her silk robe closely around her body. She gripped her throbbing head as she walked across the spacious suite to the door.

"Who is it?" she asked through the door without bothering to look through the peep hole. Irritation was evident in her voice.

"Housekeeping," answered the voice on the other side.

Disgusted, Bobbie rolled her eyes and said, "Can't you read? That sign says *do not disturb*."

"There is no sign on the door ma'am."

"Well there *should* be. I don't need no damn housekeeping!"

"Okay ma'am," the voice said, defensively.

Bobbie stomped back to the sofa and sat down. *Where the hell is Clyde?* She wondered. She looked at her cell phone again and found that there were no missed calls. Not one. She thought about dialing his number and then decided against it. She sat there a few more minutes, holding the phone as if willing it to ring, and then finally decided to take a shower and get dressed. She would have a quick breakfast or brunch and then head over to the House of Blues and pack up her dressing room. She was scheduled to leave for St. Louis the next day for the next stop on her tour.

By the time Bobbie made it outside to the taxi, it was nearly one in the afternoon and she still hadn't heard from Clyde. As she sat in the back of the cab, her eyes hidden behind a pair of Gucci sunglasses, she fought back the stinging tears. Clyde's disappearing acts had become more and more frequent lately and she just couldn't understand why. On top of that, when they were together he barely ever touched her. They barely ever made love anymore and when they did, it usually left Bobbie far from satisfied.

Most of the men in her audiences would have given anything just to touch her, and her own husband seemed so disinterested. Though she loved him, she felt like their marriage was falling apart. She had no clue as to why and wasn't sure if she could save it.

Upon arriving at the House of Blues, Bobbie paid the driver, took a deep breath, exited the cab and then walked to the building. Inside the venue, she quietly packed away her clothes, shoes, and make-up, fighting back tears the entire time. Her eyes kept diverting to the full bottle of Mariposa that sat on the floor.

She shook her head. "It's too early for that," she told herself.

She finished packing and then sat down in front of the mirror and removed her shades. "You sure don't look like no star today, Bobbie Ann," she said, referring to herself in a way reminiscent of how her mother always addressed her.

She inspected her face and rubbed her puffy eyes. She frowned at her red nose and licked her dry lips. She rubbed her hand across the paisley scarf that hid her signature afro. Sitting there in a jogging suit and no make-up, Bobbie was definitely unrecognizable, even to the most devout fan. Both her personal and professional lives were taking a toll on her.

She replaced her shades and pulled a tattered photo from the side pocket of her purse. It was a photo she'd taken with her father when she was eight-years-old. She was sitting on his knee. Both of them wore identical huge smiles.

She traced her father's face with her fingertip and said, "Daddy, I wish you were still here. I miss you so much." She wiped a single tear from her cheek. "What is a little girl supposed to do without her Daddy?"

She stared at the photo for a long while and then kissed it and tucked it away in her purse. After a thorough inspection of the room, she grabbed her bags, walked outside, hailed a cab, and headed back to the hotel.

♫♫♫

The bellman assisted Bobbie with her bags as she returned to her suite.

"Thank you," she said half-heartedly. She handed him a twenty-dollar bill. "I can get 'em now."

The bellman nodded his head and walked back to the elevator. Bobbie unlocked the door and struggled into the room with the bags to find Clyde sitting on the sofa wearing different clothes than he'd had on the day before.

"Where you been, girl?" he asked as if he'd been sitting there waiting for her for hours.

"Where the hell *you* been?!" Bobbie shrieked in response, dropping the bags with force.

"What the hell's wrong with you?" he asked. You would've thought he'd been right there in the room with her all night.

Bobbie walked closer to him, fuming. "You been out all damn night, Clyde! That's what's wrong! What kind of man just leaves his wife alone all night and don't even call her?!"

"Aw that? Baby, the car broke down. I ended up sleeping in it all night." he said matter-of-factly.

"Clyde, that's a rental. All you had to do was call the number on the key."

He shrugged his shoulders. "My phone went dead. I called 'em this morning. It's running fine now."

Bobbie shook her head. "Clyde Morgan, you a damn lie and you know it. You ain't slept in no car! I promise when I catch you into whatever you into, I'mma leave you. You can best believe that! And I'm taking all of my money with me."

"Why you coming at me like that, Bobbie?" He said, raising his voice as he stood up from the sofa. His light brown skin was now a dark shade of pink. "You threatening me? You better watch your mouth, little girl."

Bobbie stuck her neck out. "Or else what? What you think you gonna do, Clyde Morgan? I'm your meal ticket."

Clyde clenched his fists. "You know what I'm gonna do. You keep talking and I'mma show you," he said icily.

Bobbie looked at his hands and backed down. She talked a good game, but she and Clyde had fought physically before and it was not pretty. The last thing she needed to get right before a performance was a black eye or a busted lip. Those things were too hard to conceal.

She lowered her voice. "Clyde, you need to stop treating me like this. You supposed to love me. You can't keep disrespecting me like this. I'm your wife. Why can't you treat me like one?"

He frowned and held up his hand. "Don't start that mess Bobbie. You know the hell I love you. I take care of you and you ain't never had to worry about nothing, have you?"

Bobbie dropped her eyes and shook her head.

"Now, come on over here and I'll show you just how much I love you," Clyde said, his voice softer.

Bobbie walked over to Clyde and he pulled her into a sloppy kiss. *I'mma need a drink to get through this*, she thought. *But that'll just start another argument.*

She braced herself for what was Clyde's idea of lovemaking. Sometimes, Bobbie felt like he thought he was doing her a favor by having sex with her, like she should be grateful that he was giving her that much of him.

He rubbed her back as he kissed her and then stepped back and looked at her.

"See, I love you, Bobbie. Stop all that crazy talk," he said. He took her hand and led her to the bed.

A few minutes later, Bobbie lay in the bed, with the sheet wrapped around her body, and watched as Clyde walked into the bathroom in his black briefs. She closed her eyes and wondered. *Is this as good as it gets? Is this what my marriage will always be like?* To be honest, she was miserable, but she loved and depended on Clyde. He wasn't perfect but, he took care of her and had for a long time. She just didn't know if she could make it alone and she didn't want to take a chance on finding out if she could.

Clyde finally emerged from the bathroom, and Bobbie watched as he redressed.

"Where you going?" she asked.

"Girl, after that workout? I'm hungry now. I'mma go and get something to eat," he answered, without looking up from the belt buckle he was fastening.

*What workout?* She wondered. "Why don't we just order room service? We can eat in bed. Plus, I'm hungry, too."

"Naw, you know that room service is too high and we don't need to be wasting no money. I'll go and get us something." He leaned over and kissed her. "I'll be back in a little bit."

Bobbie watched as he walked out of the door knowing full well that he wouldn't be back anytime soon and that when he did return, he wouldn't have any food with him.

# THREE

### "I'm Tore Down"

IT was eleven o'clock the next morning and Clyde still had not made it back to the suite. Starving, Bobbie had eventually ordered a late dinner of filet mignon with all the trimmings from room service the previous evening. Bobbie, who usually slept until far past noon, was already awake, but there was still no sign of Clyde. With a show that night in St. Louis, she wasn't sure if she should feel angry or concerned. Sure, Clyde was known for his frequent vanishing acts; that much she was almost used to. But he'd never missed traveling with her to a show. After all, *he* was the road manager.

Bobbie checked the digital clock next to the bed again. The bright red numbers read 11:00 A.M. Her flight to St. Louis left at 2:00 P.M.

She looked at the suitcases she'd packed the night before and at the plane ticket lying on her purse. If she didn't leave for the airport soon, she'd never make it through the security checkpoints in time to make her flight. She picked up her cell phone and dialed Clyde's number for what was probably the twentieth time. Straight to voicemail. *I guess it's dead again*, she thought. Looking at her own bags, made her wonder about Clyde's luggage. *I better pack his things so they'll be ready when he gets back.* She crossed the room to the small closet. No bag. No clothes. It seemed that Clyde had already checked out.

Bobbie sat up on the side of the bed and held her head in her hands. She closed her eyes and tried to remember why she'd married Clyde in the first place.

"What were you thinking?" she asked herself aloud.

Then she shook her head and smiled. It had been Clyde who'd pulled her out of the depression she'd slid into after her father's death. Before that, it had been Clyde who'd watched over her career, making careful, calculated decisions on her behalf; and it was Clyde who'd negotiated her current record deal, one of the most lucrative in the history of recorded Delta Blues.

She was pretty successful, having sold more than a million records during her 12-year professional career. She sold out nearly every venue Clyde booked for her and she had tons of fans. All of which could be attributed to Clyde's management.

While his skills as a husband had been lacking as of recent, he had started out as a doting, loving mate. He'd been attentive and accommodating, willing to do anything for Bobbie. Bobbie smiled as she remembered how he'd proposed to her after a show in Las Vegas.

*"Little girl, I want you to be my wife. I love you,"* he'd said, while

*on bended knee in Bobbie's dressing room.*

She'd happily accepted and they had been married that same night in a small Vegas chapel. On that night, all of the pain she'd felt from her father's death some months earlier, had seemed to melt away. Clyde had become her manager, husband, and caregiver all rolled into one.

*Maybe it's just all too much for him*, she thought.

She shook her head and after a few more moments of contemplation, decided to get up, shower, and get dressed. Maybe once she was ready to leave, he'd be back. By twelve noon, Bobbie was dressed and ready to go and there was still no sign of Clyde. She sat on the sofa in the sitting area of the suite with her head in her hands, trying to figure out what to do, paralyzed by indecision. She sat there for thirty minutes before deciding to leave without him.

Dressed in black skinny jeans, a bright blue vintage Jackson Five t-shirt, and black high-heel boots, she carted the massive amount of luggage to the front desk with the assistance of a bellman.

As she approached the desk, she was greeted by a smiling brunette clerk who wore thick black slacks and a gold blouse. Her name tag read, Holly.

"How may I help you?" she asked.

"Um, I need to check out. I'm in room 1502," Bobbie replied.

"Yes, ma'am."

Bobbie handed the clerk a Visa card and drummed her fingers on the desk as she waited for her receipt.

The clerk handed the card back to her with a strange look on her face. "Um ma'am, this card was declined."

Bobbie frowned. "Really? Try this one." This time she handed her a Mastercard.

Again, the look. "Um, ma'am this one is declined too."

Shocked, Bobbie's reply was, "What?" She wondered what was going on. Clyde paid all of the bills. Had he forgotten to pay the credit card bills?

"Um, it was—" the clerk began to repeat herself.

Bobbie held up her hand and interrupted her. "I *heard* you. I just don't understand."

She looked through her wallet and found the Discover card she'd had for years. Clyde knew nothing about it since the statements were sent to her mother's house in Arkansas. She thought of it as her "emergency card".

She'd never used it before, but at that moment, she reluctantly handed it to the clerk.

The clerk swiped the card and then smiled. "Here's your receipt, ma'am."

Bobbie took the piece of paper from her. "Um, thank you." She turned to leave and then asked, "Is there a shuttle to O'Hare?" She had run out of cash and wouldn't be able to pay for a cab.

Before the clerk could answer, a man whom Bobbie hadn't noticed standing next to her said, "I'll take you, Ms. Brooks. I'm a huge fan of yours. I was at the show the other night."

Bobbie turned and looked at him. He was tall, about 6'2", with curly salt and pepper hair, expressive blue eyes and pale white skin.

He was dressed in a charcoal gray suit, white shirt, and black tie.

Bobbie guessed he could've been fifty-ish.

"Oh, uh Mr.—" she began.

"Estes. Frank Estes," he interrupted.

Bobbie gave him half of a smile. "Uh Mr. Estes, I couldn't ask you to do that. I mean, I got a bunch of luggage and I don't have any cash to pay you with."

"I've got plenty of room. It's an SUV, and uh, you can pay me with an autograph." He returned her smile.

Feeing uncertain, Bobbie's only response was, "Uh…"

She stood there for a few moments, really not sure what to do. She didn't know this man. Sure, he looked clean-cut and harmless, but looks could be very deceiving. He'd already admitted that he was a fan of hers. That alone could get really weird. But actually, what choice did she have? She could either stay there until God knows when and miss the show, disappointing her fans and risking being sued for breach of contract, or take a chance with Mr. Estes.

So she sighed and said, "Okay."

Mr. Estes, who later insisted that Bobbie address him as "Frank", helped her with her luggage and engaged her in friendly, harmless conversation all the way to the airport.

# Part Two

# Bluesday

# FOUR

### "Ain't No Love in the Heart of the City"

I arrived at the airport about thirty minutes before my flight was to leave. Frank, my hero for the moment, helped me with my bags. I gave him a hug, my autograph on the back of his hotel receipt, and a promise to make a stop in Charlotte, North Carolina (his home town) during my next tour. He was a nice guy and I was definitely grateful for the ride.

After Frank and I had parted ways, I checked my bags, sailed through security, and raced to my gate, making it just in time to board the packed plane. After a smooth flight, sandwiched in between an elderly Asian woman, who was friendly enough, and an unfriendly older black woman, I made it to Lambert International Airport in St. Louis.

I walked through the busy airport and headed directly to the ATM where I withdrew a cash advance from my "emergency card".

After I'd picked up my luggage from the corral, I walked outside and hailed a cab to Harrah's, where I would be both staying and performing.

After a ten minute ride, I'd made it to Harrah's, and I hoped that my reservation wasn't cancelled. With the way things were going, I just couldn't be for sure. I wagged to the front desk with my bags and asked the clerk if she had a reservation for a Brooks or a Morgan on file.

"Yes ma'am. Bobbie Brooks?"

I sighed with relief. "Yeah, that's me."

"Okay. Here's your key. You're in one of our luxury rooms. Enjoy your stay with us," the clerk said while smiling brightly.

"Okay, thank you."

I made my way up to the fifth floor and into the earth-tone, plush room and collapsed onto the bed. I closed my eyes, relieved that I had made it, and knew that I only had a few minutes until sound check. I took a deep breath and let it out. I heard the faint sound of my cell phone ringing. *Maybe it's Clyde*, I thought. I quickly sat up in the bed and grabbed my purse from atop the pile of bags. I dug my phone out to find that it was not Clyde, but Willie, my drummer, calling.

Will had been performing with me for five years. He was tall and husky, almost menacing in appearance, but in reality he was soft-spoken and laid-back and really just a big teddy bear. At times, he doubled as my bodyguard.

I flipped the phone open and said, "What's up Chill Will?"

"Hey, Bobbie. We got a problem."

*You telling me? I can't find my husband.* I thought, but instead I said, "What's going on?"

"Uh, Sabrina's missing. She didn't make the flight from Chicago. Camille's been tryna call her, but she ain't answering." Camille was my other back-up singer.

I frowned. "What? She didn't get on the plane with y'all?"

"Naw. We ain't seen her. I'm sorry to have to call you about this. Clyde usually handles this kinda stuff but he ain't answering either. Is he there with you?"

I gripped my forehead with my hand. I really needed a drink right about then. "No."

"Oh, well what we gonna do Bobbie?"

"Hell Will, we can't do nothing but go on. We can't cancel now. Anyway, it's not like this is the first time we've had to go on without her."

"Okay, well I'll see you at sound check then. Twenty minutes."

"Yeah, twenty minutes." I flipped my phone shut and stood up. What was with this chick? Was she *trying* to ruin me? That was it; I was firing her tail the first chance I got, no matter what Clyde had to say about it.

I walked across the room to the honor bar and searched through the tiny bottles of liquor. Jim Bean, Absolut, Bacardi, and finally, Crown Royal. I poured some Crown into one of the cups sitting next to the sink in the bathroom and gulped it down. The warm liquor burned my throat. I shook my head and closed my eyes. The show must go on.

♫♫♫

I stood behind the curtain onstage at the VooDoo Lounge with my head down and my eyes closed. I listened as the announcer screamed my name and the audience applauded. I took a sip of my drink, closed my eyes, and bobbed my head to the music as my band began to play. I was wearing tight white, ripped jeans and a red off-the-shoulder sweater, a little eighties flavor. I knew I looked good. I tapped my red high-heeled feet to the beat and as the curtain opened, I began singing the lyrics to "Messed Up", my opener, with only Camille backing me up.

 I'd decided not to worry about it. Sabrina was a lot of trouble anyway, always moody and unfriendly. Besides, these people were here to see Bobbie Brooks, *not* her back-up singers. After this show, there was only one left in New Orleans. Once the tour was finished I'd have plenty of time to find another back-up singer.

I continued to sing and rock my hips. My hair bounced as I moved across the stage grooving to the music and feeling the good vibes being sent from the crowd. Up there in front of my fans, my troubles always just seemed to melt away. I didn't think about my husband, or lack thereof. I didn't worry about the credit cards or Sabrina. I was at work. This was my job.

On stage is where my confidence was. This one thing I knew without a doubt: I was good at singing. No, I was *damn* good. Well, I should've been, I've been singing since I was eight. I grew up on the blues whether it was in the car or in the house with my daddy. Blues had surrounded me all my life. When my mama went to church, my daddy usually kept me home with him and we'd listen to Bobby

"Blue" Bland or B.B. King or Koko Taylor and sing along. There I was, this little girl singing from my heart about things I knew nothing about. For a long time I didn't know there was any other music other than the blues. Well actually, for me, I guess there really was no other type of music.

I finished "Messed Up" and took another swallow of my drink. I didn't drink all that often, but for me drinking and performing had gone hand in hand for a long while. The drink just gave me that little boost of energy I needed to get through show after show, you know, a little "liquid courage". When I wasn't on the road, I barely ever had a drink.

I swallowed hard and then said, "How y'all doing out there St. Louis?!"

I smiled as the crowd roared in response. "Alright, this next song is dedicated to my man. Any of y'all wanna be my man tonight?" The crowd roared again. I walked over to Will, who'd left his post behind the drums. Like I did at that point in every show, I chose a member of the audience to serenade. A little trick I'd picked up from Ms. Janet Jackson. Will nodded and went down into the crowd.

I'd chosen a tall, dark brown skinned brother who wore his hair in neat cornrows. He was wearing jeans and an over-sized polo. His eyes were stretched wide as Willie escorted him onstage. "Hey, be cool," Willie said into his ear. "And hands off." Willie gave him a look that said, *I'm not playing.* The guy nodded and took a seat in the chair provided for him.

I leaned in close to him and smiled seductively. "Hey baby.

What's your name?" I said into the microphone.

"Bruce," he said, eyeing me like a piece of candy.

"Well Bruce, this one's for you." I slowly and softly kissed him. I didn't usually do that, but what the hell? He looked harmless enough. The crowd roared again. Jealous men shouted comments. Bruce's eyes widened and I saw them dart towards Willie as if to say, *I didn't do it, she did.*

I gave the signal, and as Zeke began a soulful guitar intro into "So Bad", I kneeled in front of Bruce and placed my hands on his knees. I waited for the drums and keyboard to join in, and then I closed my eyes and began to sing:

*"I gotta man, he sho' does treat me bad*
*Spend all my time, alone, lonely and sad*
*Wake up at night, he's gone, don't know where*
*And when I cry he don't even seem to care*

*But I tell you this, I can't leave him alone*
*Cause his kinda lovin' is the only lovin' I know*

*Can't somebody tell me, why he treats me so bad*
*I just wanna know, what I did to make him mad*
*Please tell me, why he treats me so bad*
*If you tell me, I'll try to fix it real fast..."*

The lyrics touched my soul like they never had before and I felt something rising up inside of me. As I continued to sing, I felt the tears as they rolled down my face. I had cried plenty of times before, but this time I felt an ache I can't explain. It was almost as painful as the day my daddy died, because at that moment, I felt like my marriage had died too. I shook my head and sang the words, which echoed my real-life situation. I sang and sang until it felt like everything inside of me was emptied out, and then the song ended. I wiped my face as the audience exploded in loud applause believing that they had just witnessed a heart rending performance, not realizing that the pain I'd portrayed and tears I had shed were all too real.

I opened my eyes and Bruce was staring at me, tears in his own eyes. I'd touched him. I stood up and took his hand. I hugged him. He kept his arms beside him at first, heeding Willie's warning. Then he returned my embrace. Willie stepped forward to escort him back into the crowd.

I covered the microphone with my hand. "You here with a date?" I asked.

Bruce's eyes widened again and he shook his head. At that point, it probably wouldn't have mattered to him if he *was* with a date.

I turned to Willie. "Take him backstage." I've never done that before either.

Willie frowned. "What?"

"Take him backstage. I wanna talk to him after the show."

Willie shrugged. "It's your world. Come on, man." I watched them disappear backstage and then Willie reappeared behind the drums.

"Alright, now that I got me a man, let's party, y'all!" I screamed.

The crowd seemed more than willing to party with me. I continued my show, one of my best, I must say, and then headed backstage to my dressing room.

Bruce was standing just beyond the curtains, where he'd watched the remainder of the show. I grabbed his hand and led him to my dressing room. I closed the door behind us and pushed him onto the small loveseat. He looked at me like it was the first time he'd seen a woman, like he'd discovered some new, wonderful treasure.

"How old are you, Bruce?" I asked as I straddled his lap.

"Uh…uh twenty?" he said as if he wasn't at all sure.

"Really? Young for a blues fan, ain't you?" I said as my lips hovered over his.

"Uh, my…my mama likes blues." I guess he meant that she'd turned him onto the blues, like my daddy had me.

I inspected his face. In the dim light of the dressing room, he looked even younger than twenty. Smooth brown skin and the shadow of a mustache gave him away. Eighteen maybe? Whatever. It didn't matter.

I kissed Bruce, hard this time. He sat there, stiff as a board at first, and then instinct kicked in. He placed his hands on my hips and began to kiss me back. He wasn't a half-bad kisser either. I wrapped my arms around him and waited for my better judgment to kick in. I waited for the voice in my head to tell me to stop, that I was a married woman, and that this was wrong. I never heard it. I ended the kiss and looked at Bruce. He was breathing hard. I don't know if it was the liquor, or the fact that I just needed someone, but I kissed him again. This time, he placed his hands on my back and eased them down to my behind. I didn't stop him. I undressed him, still listening closely for that voice of reason to shout at me. Silence. I gave Bruce what every other male fan wanted. I gave him a night he'd never forget, a story he'd tell over and over again like an old soldier telling war stories.

I took my sweet time and seduced him in my dressing room, and then I took him up to my suite and seduced him two more times.

Maybe I wanted Clyde to catch me. I don't know. All I know is that when Bruce left my suite the next morning, he was wearing a big smile and the scent of my Beyoncé Heat cologne all over his body. With an autographed CD in hand, he thanked me and headed out the door. In my hand, I held a slip of paper with his phone number. I looked across the room at the trash can which held empty foil wrappers, the only evidence of the night before. I sat on the side of the bed and cried.

# FIVE

### "Members Only"

I unlocked the front door to the dark red bricked townhouse that Clyde and I had shared for a little more than four years. The tour was over. I'd left New Orleans after a sold-out show with another one-night stand under my belt and another phone number in my pocket, *just in case*. Up until that night in St. Louis, I'd only been with one man other than Clyde my whole life. I had doubled my number of partners in less than a week.

I hadn't heard from Clyde since Chicago. I'd stopped trying to call his phone. Wherever he was and whatever he was doing, he sure didn't seem to be concerned about my wellbeing. I had virtually no money and had skated through the end of the tour using my emergency card, which was fast approaching its limit. I didn't understand why he constantly mistreated me or why he'd deserted me or at least it seemed that he had.

I tried to be a good wife. Basically, I was the breadwinner of the family, and I had never complained about it. Not once.

I walked into the foyer and set my bags down on the shiny marble floor. I bent over and picked up the mountain of mail that had accumulated behind the door beneath the brass mail slot. I placed the pile on the cherry wood table that sat beside the staircase and sighed. *Clyde'll take care of them when he gets here*, I thought. *Probably just bills, anyway.* I glanced above the table at the wedding portrait that hung on the wall. I quickly looked away. It hurt to see our smiling faces.

I dragged my bags up the beige carpeted stairs to our bedroom. I slid the closet door open and gasped. Every stitch of Clyde's clothing was gone. Every suit, every shirt, every pair of pants, gone. I dropped my eyes to the floor. Missing were the many pairs of shiny, expensive shoes that he owned. I rushed across the room to first the dresser and then the chest. His drawers were empty. His toiletries were even missing from the bathroom. When had he done this? When I was still out on the road? Had he planned it all?

I fell across the bed and buried my face in the black satin comforter, which provided absolutely no comfort at that moment. He was actually gone. It wasn't unusual for him to leave and stay gone for days at a time, but this time he'd actually taken his clothes.

What was I going to do? I'd never paid a single bill in my life. I couldn't even tell you what a bill looked like. I never read any contracts. I just signed whatever Clyde put in front of me. What in the world was I going to do? I'd always had someone to take care of me, whether it was my daddy or Clyde. Now, I had no one.

I laid there and cried and cried until I ran out of tears, and then I just laid there and stared at the half-empty closet. I laid there for what seemed like days but was in reality a few hours, ignoring the ringing telephone and knocks at the door, until I fell asleep.

♫♫♫

The next morning I laid there and listened as someone knocked at the door and then repeatedly rang the doorbell. I looked over at the clock on the bedside table. It read eleven o'clock. At that point, I had no idea if it was A.M. or P.M. I peered at the window behind the headboard and saw sunlight peeking in between the slots of the mini blind.

I wiped my cheek as I sat up in the bed. I was crying again and my head throbbed as I slowly made my way down the stairs to answer the door. Heaven only knows how I must've looked at that point. I'm sure that I was truly a sight to see since I'd been crying off and on for hours. I finally reached the door and opened it without looking through the peep hole and stared at the wide Hispanic man who stood on the other side. He wore stiffly starched khaki pants and an equally board-like royal blue shirt. Clipped to his belt was some type of badge. Dallas P.D.? Sherriff's department?

"Ms. Brooks?" He asked.

"Yes," I answered vacantly, my eyelids heavy.

"You've been served," he said, then handed me a large brown envelope and turned to leave. I backed into the foyer and closed the door behind me.

I ripped open the envelope and pulled out the neatly bound papers. I slowly read the first few lines of the first page.

### The District Court of Dallas County, Texas
### 254th District Court
### Petition for Divorce

**Petitioner: Clyde Marvin Morgan**

**Respondent: Bobbie BluAnn Brooks**

That was all I managed to read before I dropped the papers on the floor and then turned and walked back up the stairs to my bedroom where I fell across my bed, but this time I didn't cry. *I need a drink*, I thought. *Yeah, I'll feel better after a drink.* I sat up in the bed, ignored the ringing of the telephone, then stood and walked over to the dresser. I pulled open the drawer where I had hidden a full bottle of whisky. I had hidden it because I was tired of Clyde telling me I didn't need to drink at home. Once upon a time, he'd thought that it was okay to drink on the road; whatever it took to make a good performance. But the more I drank, the more he seemed to change his mind about it. He especially hated for me drink at home. He said it made me too loose.

"Well Clyde ain't here," I told myself and turned the bottle up. I laughed to myself as I thought about a popular song I'd heard on the radio, *Bottoms up, indeed,* I thought. I tipped the bottle again.

Another swallow.

I shuddered as the warm liquor burned my throat. I sat on the bed and then slid to the floor. I drank and drank until the bottle was empty and then I went into the bathroom, reached under the sink and found another hidden bottle.

It wasn't long before I had finished it as well. I staggered to my feet and stumbled downstairs to the kitchen, reached into the back of the pantry, and found bottles number three and four. I sat in a chair at the table and continued my one-woman party. *It's a private party, alright.*

I raised the last bottle to my lips and said, "Here's to Clyde." As the liquor slid down my throat, everything went black.

# SIX

### "St. James Infirmary"

I opened my eyes and then quickly shut them as the bright lights above my head nearly blinded me. *Is this the light I heard about? Is this heaven?*

I smiled. "Thank God it's over," I whispered.

"Did you say somethin', Bobbie Ann?" It was my mother's voice. I opened my eyes to see that she was standing over me, her small, dark eyes full of concern.

"Mama? You in heaven too?" I asked, confused.

Mama patted my shoulder. "Bobbie Ann! Bobbie Ann, you in a hospital, in Dallas."

"Oh no! What happened?" Tears began to fill my closed eyes. I was scared and even more so, confused. With the tears came a dull, nagging headache. My teeth hurt, too.

"Bobbie Ann, look at me," Mama said sternly. I peered at her through squinted eyes. Although we'd never been very close, I'd always thought that my mama was a beautiful woman. She was short and petite, almost fragile, but her presence had always made her seem ten feet tall to me.

"Yes ma'am?" I said weakly.

"You got alcohol poisonin'. You almost drank yo' self ta death. Was you tryna' kill yo' self? You know dat's a sin dontcha?" She asked with a southern accent so thick that it almost sounded like a foreign language.

I closed my eyes and shook my head. "I don't know what I meant to do. I just wanted the hurt to go away."

"Clyde done leff' ya?"

I nodded and blinked back more tears. "Yes ma'am, he did."

Mama looked down at me with a stern expression. "Humph. I say good riddance to 'em. He won't no good no way."

I wiped my face as the tears began to spill. "But he's my husband, Mama. He ain't no good, but I still love him. I miss him, and I need him."

She looked away from me and straightened the front of her patterned green blouse. "Well, no since in whinin' and cryin'. He gone now. You need ta straighten 'yo self out." That was my mama. As far as she was concerned, there was never any time for emotional nonsense. A woman was supposed to be tough, take things as they came to her, and move on.

I nodded and pushed myself up in the bed. I looked down at the standard white hospital gown decorated with tiny blue squares which covered my body and at the ID bracelet on my left wrist. "How long've I been in here? Who brought me here?" I asked.

Mama sat in the chair next to the bed and rubbed her hands across the thighs of her navy-blue, knit pants. "Well, they say da maid found cha. Say you was on da kitchen flo' barely breathin', so she cawled 911. You been here two days. They found my number in yo' purse and cawled me. I got here dis mornin'. Kevin took me ta Texarkana, and I rode da bus here." Kevin was one of my cousins; my Aunt Werdine's only son.

I rubbed my head and felt my matted hair. "What time is it now?"

"Twelve noon. Doctor say you can go home in a coupla days but you can't be alone."

"Oh, um okay."

"He say you gone need some counselin' too. You gone have ta come home wit me. I can't stay here in Dallas. I still got Meka and Sharee ta see at." Tomeka and Sharee were my brother's daughters. Mama had been raising them ever since they were four and five. My brother, Junior and their mother, Nora Lee, had both been strung out on drugs for years.

"I'm okay Mama. I'll be okay. I'll stay here in Dallas, and you can go on back to the girls."

"It's me and couselin' or you gotta go ta one of dem places," she replied.

I frowned. "You mean like a Rehab center?"

"Yeah, dat's what tha doctor said. What chu gone do?"

I didn't like my mother very much and we didn't get along at all, but if I had to choose between her and a building full of loons, I chose her. I ain't no Lindsay Lohan. "I'll go with you, then," I said softly.

"Now when they let you leave, we'll go by yo' house and get some uh yo' things. Then we'll take da bus back to Arkansas."

I shook my head. "I have a car. I can drive us."

"If da doctor say it's okay, den fine."

"Yes ma'am."

"Well, I'll be over here if ya need me. You howngry?"

I nodded. "Yes ma'am."

"Okay, lemme go tell da nurse."

I nodded and after she'd left the room, I closed my eyes and sighed. I hadn't seen my mama in four years before that day. What a reunion.

♫♫♫

I took the last bag to my Escalade and shut the back gate. Mama had already climbed into the passenger side and was eyeing the interior of the truck with wide eyes. I climbed into the driver's seat and started the engine.

"Bobbie Ann? When you get dis van? You ain't have dis da last time you came home didya?"

I shook my head. "No ma'am. I had a car. A Mustang. This is a Cadillac SUV."

"Humph. Sho' is fancy enough. You got a TV in here. Lawd have mercy."

I smiled. "Mama, I need to go by the bank first and then we can head home."

She shrugged her shoulders. "Whatever you need ta do. I just need ta get back ta dem girls. Werdine keepin' em and you know she don't really like other folks' kids."

"Yes ma'am. I'll be quick. It shouldn't take long at all."

Twenty minutes later, I pulled in front of a small branch office of The First Bank of Texas and parked.

"I'll be right back," I said and then jumped out of the truck. I walked inside and found that luckily, there was no line. I stepped in front of a teller and handed her the check I'd written for cash.

"How are you, Ms. Brooks?" She asked with a smile.

She was a tall, thin young lady with medium brown skin and blond micro braids. She wore way too much make-up, but her smile was infectious. I'd never seen her before so she must have read my name on the check. Her name tag read Tiffany.

"Fine, thanks." I said and watched as she pecked at the computer keyboard and then noticed a frown spread across her face. *Not again*, I thought.

"What's wrong," I asked.

"Well, um, this account has been closed, Ms. Brooks."

"What?!"

She looked up at me with a helpless expression. "That's what it says here, ma'am," she said as she pointed to the computer screen.

I held my forehead. "What is going on?!"

I think I startled the teller because her expression quickly changed to one of fear. "Would you like for me to get the manager, ma'am?"

I nodded. "Yes, please."

A few minutes later, I found myself sitting in a glass-enclosed office across from the stiff branch manager. She was an older red-headed white woman with wrinkled skin who wore no make-up at all. She really could have used some of Tiffany's. She wore a drab gray pant suit and black orthopedic shoes. She peered over her rectangular glasses as she leaned forward and spoke to me.

"Well Ms. Brooks, it seems that you closed all of your accounts here, with exception of your savings account, about a week ago," she said.

Well that figured, my savings account was the only one that Clyde didn't know about or have access to.

I shook my head. "No ma'am. I didn't close anything. I wasn't even in town then. Those were joint accounts. My husband must've closed them."

She nodded. "Yes, he was the one who came in and made the final withdrawals, but he presented a request for closure with your signature on it. See."

She handed me the forms. Sure enough, my sloppy signature was on every one of them. Clyde had used my trust in him against me. He knew I'd sign anything he placed in front of me without reading it.

I slapped the papers against my lap. "But, my royalties are deposited into those accounts."

"Ms. Brooks, all I can tell you is that all of the accounts have been closed. As far as royalties, I have no idea."

I sat silently for a moment and then stood up from the uncomfortable brown leather chair. "Sorry to bother you," I said softly, "I'm gonna need to take the money out of my savings, then."

"Certainly, Ms. Brooks. Just a moment."

Ten minutes later, I emerged from the bank, pale-faced and furious. I climbed into the truck and pulled out my cell phone.

"Bobbie Ann, what's wrong? Who you callin'?" Mama asked with a concerned expression.

"Clyde."

I dialed the number. Straight to voicemail, of course.

Once the tone had sounded in my ear, I yelled into the phone, "Clyde, you son-of-a—" I remembered Mama was sitting next to me and cut myself off. "Clyde, I know you ignoring my calls," I continued. "I don't care about you or whatever tramp you with, but I *do* care about my money. You stole my money you piece of crap and you gone get it!" I ended the call and then scrolled through my phone contacts.

"Oh, Lawd. Calm down, Bobbie Ann! Who you callin' now?" Mama said, alarm written all over her face.

"I'm calling my lawyer to find out if he knows where my royalties are going now."

"Royalties?" Mama asked sounding confused.

"The money they pay me for album sales, concerts, just about anything I do that *makes* money. *My work*."

"Is it a lot?"

I nodded. "Yes ma'am, and I'm not letting Clyde steal it all from me."

I finally found Carl Golden's number and dialed it. I tapped my fingers on the steering wheel as I waited for the receptionist to answer.

"Parker, Smith, and Golden," she answered, brightly.

"Yes, this is Bobbie Brooks. I need to speak with Mr. Golden."

"One moment."

I waited until he finally answered in his thick Midwestern accent. "Ms. Brooks! How can I help you on this Friday afternoon?"

"First of all, I need you to draw up something saying that Clyde Morgan is no longer my manager."

"Oh, okay," he said, sounding a little startled, "I just talked to him the other day. He brought me a letter from you."

"Well, that's strange since I haven't seen him in weeks."

"Oh, well, it has your signature."

I shook my head. I was so freakin' stupid! "I imagine it does. What's it say?"

"Um, that you want your royalties deposited into a different account. I was just about to have my secretary send out the notices."

"Well don't. Let me give you another account number."

"I'll need it in writing Ms. Brooks."

"Fine. I'll take care of it. I'll be at my mother's in Arkansas for a while. Let me give you the phone number and address." I rattled off the number and address and told him I'd get a letter to him in a few days.

"Okay. Got it. Um, Ms. Brooks, I heard you weren't feeling well. I hope you're feeling better."

"I will be." I hung up and started the car.

Mama shook her head and let out a quiet, "Humph."

I looked over at her. "What does that mean?" I wasn't in the mood for her.

"So you ready ta fight now, huh? You willing ta fight over money ain't cha."

I sighed and fought hard not to roll my eyes. "Mama, if you knew how hard I worked for that money, you'd be fighting too."

She answered with another "Humph."

A few minutes later, me and Mama were on I-30 East headed to Arkansas and rode most of the way in total silence.

# SEVEN

## "Down Home Blues"

I pulled my electric blue Escalade onto the gravel path that led from the main road to the driveway of my mother's home. A smile crept upon my lips as the familiar white frame house came into view. It was surrounded by a white picket fence and stood far back off of the road. Behind it I could see a grove of pine and oak trees. I saw the rose bushes that my father had planted in front of the house when I was a little girl. They had grown so tall that they now hid the bottom of the front porch. Mama's favorite old wooden glider sat on the porch along with two dusty yard chairs.

I turned onto the red clay dirt driveway. Under the carport I could see my daddy's old red Chevy truck sitting there giving the illusion that he was inside, rocking in his chair listening to his favorite records.

I took a deep breath and fought back tears as I noticed the old swing set I used to play on sitting to the side of the house. Once painted a bright yellow, it was now a dull rust color and looked as if it might collapse at any moment. Across the property sat Willisville Baptist Church. It was my Mama's church, and it was sitting on part of our family's land. I smiled again as I remembered playing hide and seek behind the church and hearing the small choir practice on Saturday mornings.

"We're here," I said without even realizing that I was speaking aloud.

"Yeah, we are." Mama said, matter-of-factly.

I parked next to her gray Buick, a car she'd had for at least twenty years, having refused to let me buy her another one.

"Well, come on in," she said as she slid out of the truck with a grunt. "You can have da' front bedroom. Meka and Sharee got yo' old room."

"Yes ma'am," I said as I walked around to the back of the truck to get my bags.

We entered through the side door which led directly into the small den. As I stepped into the house, I felt as if I'd travelled into the past. I saw the same navy blue and beige floral patterned couch and matching chair, the same old floor-model TV, the same decorative wall hangings all coordinated to match. The only difference was that the room looked like it had recently been painted. I could still smell the bacon she'd cooked for breakfast before leaving for Dallas.

I followed her into the small bedroom just off the den. In it was a full-sized bed with probably five mattresses stacked on it. My mama never threw *anything* away. There was an antique dresser and matching high-boy. The room was so small that I had to navigate my way around the three pieces of furniture and was actually afraid I'd knock down one of Mama's what-nots and break it. I sat my bags on the bed and watched it jiggle in response. Sleeping in it would certainly be interesting.

"Around here dinner's at seven. We all in bed by nine and we up by six. I know you paid dis house off and I thanks you, but while you here, you gone have ta help out. Ain't no maid service and ain't no room service," Mama said, as if she was listing the rules for a halfway house. Around my mama, I instantly felt like a little girl again. Like if I talked back or sassed her, she'd grab one of my daddy's thick leather belts and tear my hide up.

So, I just said, "Okay, yes ma'am."

"And give me yo' keys."

I frowned. "What?"

She put her hands on her hips and raised her eyebrows. "Did I stutter? You ain't sneakin' back ta Dallas. All dat fast livin' what got you where you at now." She held out her hand and added, "*Keys*, Bobbie Ann."

"But—" I began to speak then cut myself off. What was the use? I handed her my keys.

"Okay, now you gone and get settled. When you git done in here, you can help me in da kitchen. Werdine'll be here after while wit' da girls."

I sighed. "Yes ma'am."

She turned to leave and then stopped in her tracks and said, "And we go ta church on Sunday. *Every Sunday*."

She was just taking things too far. "Now Mama, I ain't been to church in years. I don't think they'll want me there with me being a blues singer. You know?"

"I shoulda made you go when you was a girl, but yo' daddy—" She shook her head. "Anyway, you goin'. Don't matter whether or not you want to."

I closed my eyes and sighed. "*Okay*, Mama."

"Humph, I know it's okay. Can't be nothin' *but* okay." She turned and left.

I fell across the bed and felt like I was floating on water. *Oh boy*, I thought. *Here we go.*

♫♫♫

I sat across the dinner table and smiled at Tomeka and Sharee as they whispered and giggled with one another. After a few more minutes of hushed conversation, it was Tomeka who finally spoke up.

"Aunt Bobbie Ann?" she asked.

"Yes?" I answered.

"You ever met Lil' Wayne?" She asked with her tiny eyes open wide.

She was a beautiful thirteen-year-old with dark brown skin and bone structure just like Mama's. Her pressed hair was pulled back into a tight ponytail. She was tall and thin like my brother and my daddy.

"Who's Lou Wayne?" Mama asked, clearly annoyed by the question.

"Not Lou Wayne, Granny. *Lil'* Wayne," Tomeka said.

"Lou Wayne, Lil' Wayne, whatever. What is he? A cowboy or somethin'? He some kin ta John Wayne?"

Sharee asked, "Who is John Wayne?" as if it were the most ridiculous name she'd ever heard. She was a year younger than her sister and her skin was a shade lighter. Her thick sandy hair and brown eyes were like her mother's. If Tomeka resembled Junior at all then Sharee certainly resembled Nora Lee.

I smiled and shook my head. "No ma'am, he's a rapper." I turned to Sharee. "And John Wayne was an actor. He was in a lot of cowboy movies."

Mama rolled her eyes. "A rapper?! That old rap mess is worser dan da blues. It's all from da devil if ya ask me."

I stopped smiling and turned back to the girls. "Um, no I never met him, but he was at a party I was at one time."

"Wow," they said in unison.

Mama looked at me. "Don't be fillin'they heads wit' dat mess. Parties and liquor and all dat. That mess didn't do nothin' but ruin yo' life," she snapped. Then she turned to the girls and said, "Y'all finish yo' dinner and wash da dishes. You got choir practice in da mornin'."

"Yes ma'am," they said, again in unison.

I smiled at them and they smiled back. We finished dinner with no further discussion of rap or blues.

After dinner, I went into my bedroom, changed into my nightgown, and hoisted myself onto the bed. I pulled the covers over my body and closed my eyes.

"Goodnight, Bobbie Ann," I told myself and then drifted off to sleep, dreaming of oceans and boats all night long. Seriously, I did.

# EIGHT

### "Sweet Sixteen"

EVIDENTLY Mama was actually serious about the whole "up by six" thing, because at five after six the next morning, she came into the room where I was asleep and shook me until I opened my eyes.

I rolled over with a frown and a slight headache and squinted up at her. "Ma'am?"

"It's after six. Get up and get yo' self together. I'll be in da kitchen." With that, she turned and left, her purple caftan flowing behind her, pink and blue magnetic rollers in her hair.

I raised myself up on my elbows and wondered what in the world was right about getting up at that hour on a Saturday morning.

After a few moments of silent complaining, I rolled out of bed, wrapped my robe around me, and stumbled through the den and into the small hallway that led to the even smaller bathroom. I swear I must've had motion sickness. Anyway, once I reached my destination, there was barely enough room to maneuver in the tiny bathroom with just a toilet, face bowl, and tub, no shower. By the time I'd used the toilet and washed my hands and face, it was already six-thirty. I left the bathroom and slowly made my way to the kitchen. Mama was already at the stove frying what smelled like bacon. The aroma was heavenly. Mama didn't notice me standing in the doorway.

"Um, I'm here. You need me to do something?" I asked.

Mama didn't look up from the stove. "You can mix up some eggs for scramblin'. You remember how, don'tcha?"

I nodded. "Yes ma'am," I said through a yawn and then gathered everything I'd need.

About thirty minutes later, Mama, Meka, Sharee, and I sat down for a breakfast of bacon, scrambled eggs, biscuits, cheese grits, and fried potatoes. I must admit; it was the best breakfast I'd eaten in years.

After breakfast, we all took turns in the bathroom taking baths, beginning with Meka and ending with Mama. I dressed in a pair of faded jeans, an old tour t-shirt of mine, and sneakers; appropriate wear for the early September weather. I made my bed and decided to clean the kitchen up for Mama. By the time Mama was finished getting dressed and had walked into the kitchen, it was squeaky clean.

Her eyes widened. "You did dis by yo' self?"

I smiled proudly. "Yes ma'am."

"Humph. I figured you forgot how ta clean up since ya been so busy livin' it up."

I dropped my smile and my eyes.

"Anyway, me and Werdine's goin' to da flea market and some rummage sales. You can go if you want to."

I shook my head. "No, thank you. I'll just hang around here." I didn't feel like being around Aunt Werdine or anyone else for that matter.

"Well, suit yo' self. Just be sho' and walk the girls over to the church for choir practice by nine."

"But—"

She raised her hand. "You ain't gotta stay. Just make sho' they go inside."

"Yes ma'am."

Right about then I heard a car horn honk.

She started walking out of the kitchen. "That's Werdine. I'll be back by noon, and we can fix lunch," she said as she pulled the strap of her huge black purse over her shoulder. She was wearing a pair of brown knit pants, a beige blouse, and brown moccasins.

"Ok, Mama."

She left, and I walked back into the bedroom and unplugged my phone from the charger. *Wonder how much longer before it's cut off*, I thought. Yes, Clyde handled that bill, too. I checked the screen — no missed calls, although, I really don't know who I expected to call me. I had no friends except my band members, and it was Saturday, so there would be no business calls. I sighed and then dug a notebook out of one of my bags. If nothing else, maybe some good songs would come out of this whole mess.

♫♫♫

At 8:50 A.M., I headed across the front yard to the church with the girls. We made it there right before choir rehearsal began, and I watched as the two sisters walked happily up the front steps and into the church. I waited for the door to shut behind them and then turned to walk back to the house. I had made it to the edge of the carport when I heard the sound of a car's engine behind me. I didn't bother to turn around, figuring that it was probably just one of those nosy ladies from the church wanting to butt into my business. I fought the urge to flip them a birdie. *Nosy old biddies.*

I was almost back at the house when I heard the car stop and then a voice said, "Excuse me ma'am. Is Ms. Mae Brooks home?"

I stopped dead in my tracks. The voice was deeper, more mature, but I recognized it. It had the same effect on me at that moment as it had years earlier; butterflies flooded my stomach, and my breath quickened. I slowly turned in the direction of the vehicle and saw him. He stuck his head out of the window as he continued to speak.

"Bobbie Ann, that you?" He seemed just as shocked to see me as I was to see him.

"Reggie?" I asked without answering his question, but of course I knew it was him. The statement was more of an expression of my surprise to see him than an actual question requiring an answer.

He opened the door and stepped out of the dusty white Yukon. I thought I would faint, right then and there. He was just as handsome as ever. No, actually, I think he may have improved with age. He stood about 6'7" tall with smooth skin the color of creamy milk chocolate. His face was adorned with large, round, hazel eyes, bushy eyebrows, and full lips. Atop his head was a crop of curly black hair which was cut short. He wore loose-fitting, dark blue jeans and a light blue oxford shirt. His body had fully developed into that of a grown man. The years I'd missed seeing him had done him good. Just as he had managed to do so many years before, Reggie Darrough had taken my breath away.

His thick lips parted to reveal a bright white smile as he looked me up and down. He could see that I'd developed, too. "Bobbie Ann! It's been a long time, Superstar." "Superstar" had always been his special nickname for me. He had always pegged me for greatness.

I swallowed hard and nodded. "Twelve years," I said, barely above a whisper. I held my hand to my chest. My mouth felt dry.

"Yeah," he said as he moved closer to me. "I know you're a married woman, but can I have a hug?"

"Not for long," I muttered, my eyes fixed on his.

He looked confused. "I don't mind a short hug."

He'd obviously misunderstood me. I shook my head. "No, I mean I won't be married for long. It seems that we're getting a divorce."

He moved even closer and pulled me into a tight hug. I nearly melted right there in his arms. He felt so strong, so powerful, and after all those years, it still felt familiar to be in his arms. I'd nearly forgotten what it felt like for a man to hold me like that. I could smell the fabric softener on his shirt as I closed my eyes and took a deep breath.

"I'm sorry to hear that, Bobbie Ann. I really am," he said sincerely.

He released me, and I answered with a weak, "Thanks." I ran my fingers through my soft afro. "Um, Mama's gone with Aunt Werdine. You were looking for her?"

He nodded and stuck his hands in the back pockets of his jeans, allowing his muscular chest to stick out. "Uh, yeah. I promised to take a look at her washing machine. She says it's leaking."

I cleared my throat and averted my attention from his chest to his face. "Oh, well come on. I was heading back in the house anyway."

He smiled. "What? No choir practice for you? I know you still got that voice, girl."

I shook my head. "Naw, I doubt if they want a blues-singing heathen in the choir, you know? That might cause some problems."

He gave me a serious look. "They don't think that about you, Bobbie Ann."

I raised my eyebrows. "Yeah they do, my mama included."

His brow wrinkled. "Bobbie Ann, don't say that."

I shrugged. "It's the truth. Anyway, come on in."

Reggie shook his head and followed me into the house, out the back door, and the few feet into the backyard to the shed, where the washer and dryer were located. I left him to do his work and went back into the house. I grabbed my notebook since I'd planned on doing some writing. However, my mind stayed on Reggie and those eyes. I finally went into the kitchen and poured a huge glass of iced tea. I walked back out to the shed and saw that Reggie had pulled the washer from the wall. He was leaning over looking into the drain with a flashlight. He didn't notice me standing there staring at him.

"You thirsty?" I asked, holding up the cup.

He turned and smiled at me. I quickly looked away, afraid my eyes would betray me.

"That some of Ms. Mae's tea?" he asked.

I nodded and then handed him the cup. He nearly drank it all in one gulp.

He rubbed his stomach and said, "Your mama still makes the best tea in the world and I should know."

"Yeah, what you doing here in Willisville, Arkansas being Mr. Fix-it? I thought you were still playing ball overseas. "

He shrugged. "My mama got sick so I came home about six months ago to take care of her."

"Oh, how is she?" Reggie was Ms. Cassie Darrough's only child and a Mama's boy to his heart.

"She's better. It's her diabetes. She's so hard-headed when it comes to getting her to eat right and take care of herself."

"Well I'm glad she's doing better. Um, is your wife here too?" *I hope not because I sure am enjoying looking at her husband.*

"Nope," he said abruptly.

"Oh. Okay." I guess she wasn't up for discussion. "Um, sorry to bother you. I'll let you finish." I turned to leave.

"We're not together anymore," he said.

I turned back around and looked at him. He was leaning over the drain again. "Oh, I'm sorry," I said.

He looked up at me. "It's alright. It was for the best. I know that now."

"But didn't y'all have kids?"

He dropped his eyes. "Uh, yeah."

"I'm really sorry Reggie. I truly am."

"Thanks."

I waved my hands and said, "Let me leave you alone. I'm hindering your work."

He held his hand up. "Naw, I'm done," he said as he effortlessly pushed the machine back against the wall. "Tell your mama that the line is clogged. Probably some lint or a sock or something. I'll be back tomorrow after church with some drain opener. That should take care of it. You going to church?"

I nodded and rolled my eyes. "Yeah, against my will."

He laughed. "Good. I'll see you there, then."

"Okay."

# NINE

### "Preaching the Blues"

I smoothed the front of my shear white blouse and sighed. Under it I wore a black camisole but that still had not satisfied my mother's critical eye. After I'd emerged from my bedroom dressed in the blouse, a black pencil skirt that fell right at my knees, three inch black heels, and silver hoop earrings, her only response had been her usual, "Humph" followed by "Don't chu got a jacket you can put on?"

I wordlessly re-entered the bedroom, grabbed a short black leather jacket, and shrugged into it. Being as this was the most conservative outfit I could come up with, I was in bad shape for future Sundays.

When I returned, she simply shook her head, sighed, and said, "Let's go."

I rubbed my hand across my hair, which I had swept to one side using bobby pins, and wondered if maybe it was too much for church. Well, it was too late to worry about that, because Mama was headed out the door with Meka and Sharee, both dressed in white blouses and black skirts, right behind her. If I didn't follow suit, I'd never hear the end of it. I followed them out the door, pulling it shut behind me.

I followed them across the yard to the church. I could see the other church-goers entering the building. I felt more and more self-conscious with every step. I hadn't been near a church since the day I married Clyde, and actually, that was just a little chapel in Vegas.

I walked up the concrete steps covered in green indoor/outdoor carpet, and once I reached the top step, I froze. I hesitated at the door and I felt my stomach drop. *I can't do this,* I thought. *I can't go in there.* I stood there and stared at the glass double doors leading into the church and nearly turned to leave. Mama turned and gave me one of her "looks" and I finally followed her into the small entryway which was decorated with colorful artificial flowers. A gold cross hung on one wall and on the opposite wall there was a black board with magnetic letters, outlining the times of the various services held at the church.

We entered the sanctuary through the two wooden doors which separated it from the entry way, and I felt like time in the little church had stopped. The same burgundy carpet and curtains, the same wooden pews (ten on each side), the amen corner to the left of the pulpit, the mother's bench to the right. It appeared as if absolutely nothing had changed.

Several mismatched chairs lined the half-wall of the pulpit. The nicest chair was situated directly behind the podium. It was reserved for the pastor. The small choir stand stood directly behind the pulpit and could seat about a dozen people, max. Behind it was the only new addition to the church; a baptismal pool with a lighted picture of the last supper overlooking it.

Heads turned and tongues wagged as I followed Mama down the center aisle. Mama smiled and waved at the other members who in turn smiled and waved back at her and then eyed me from head to toe. Finally, after what seemed like an endless march down the short aisle, Mama slid onto a pew second from the front and to the right of the pulpit. I took a seat next to her and tugged at my skirt which rode up my thigh after I sat down. Mama glanced at me and then turned to speak to a lady who didn't look familiar to me.

"Good morning Sista' Brooks," said the heavy-set, brown-skinned woman dressed in a hideous floral print purple dress. As she spoke, she stared at me.

"Good mornin', Essie Jean. You remember Bobbie Ann?" Mama replied and then gestured towards me.

"This is little Bobbie Ann? Well, hey there!" She extended her hand to me.

I smiled and offered her a quiet, "Hi." I shook her hand but had no idea who she was.

As if reading my mind, Mama said, "Essie used ta work up at da school wit' me." Mama had been working in the school cafeteria ever since I could remember.

I nodded. "Oh, good to see you, Ms. Essie." Of course, I still didn't remember who she was.

Before Ms. Essie could reply, the pianist began to play, signaling the start of the service. I smiled at the sight of Meka and Sharee, who along with a few other children dressed in black and white, filled the small choir stand. Soon the children's voices joined the pianist as they began to sing "Up Above My Head." I clapped along with the music and felt a little of my self-consciousness begin to melt away. I guess music just had a way of relaxing me.

The song ended and Deacon Jones and Deacon Willis stepped over to the announcer's podium in front of the mother's bench, and began devotion. I swear those two had to be at least a hundred years old because I could remember them being old when I was a little girl. I softly joined the congregational hymn and then bowed my head with closed eyes for the prayer.

Prayer ended with a unanimous "amen". I opened my eyes and lifted my head and nearly fainted. Pastor Arnold was leading a line of preachers into the sanctuary from one of the side doors and as I watched the small procession, my mouth dropped open. Behind him were several men I did not recognize, but the last preacher, I recognized well.

Reggie Darrough stepped into the pulpit wearing a nice navy blue suit, white shirt, and navy blue tie. He claimed the last seat; the one furthest to the right, of course. Several questions ran through my mind and distracted me from the service. Reggie's a preacher? I couldn't believe it. Not that he was a bad person or anything like that. On the contrary, he was always a good person, but a preacher? I just didn't see that one coming. I was itching to ask Mama about

Reggie being a preacher but I was sure she'd only give me the evil eye for whispering during church service.

As the service continued, I found myself staring at him, and a few times I think I noticed him looking at me as well. To say I'd been in love with Reggie was an understatement. We had dated for two years from the time I was only sixteen years-old. Our relationship had abruptly ended when he left for college in Fayetteville, and shortly thereafter I landed my first record deal and began recording and travelling all over the country. But in those two years we were together, we'd loved each other enough for two lifetimes.

Bound together by the shared angst of strained family relationships, (his with his absent father and mine with my cold mother) we spent most of our time together comforting each other. We shared our individual secrets and dreams and made plans for a future together that never came to pass. When we separated, although I was living my dream as a performer, my heart ached for him and what could've been. Though I did love Clyde, what I felt for him was nothing compared to what I'd felt for Reggie Darrough.

I snapped out of my thoughts and quickly dug a ten-dollar bill out of my purse as I noticed the collection plate fast approaching me. Moments later, I stood with the rest of the congregation and sang the preparatory hymn, "Amazing Grace". Afterwards, we took our seats and listened as Pastor Arnold began to speak.

"Good morning, Saints," he said with the voice of a televangelist. He was a short, dark-skinned man with strong features and thick graying hair that he wore in a short neat afro.

"Good morning," the congregation replied, poised to turn their Bibles to whichever scripture he directed them to.

"This morning, I'd like for you all to welcome one of our own. I asked Reverend Darrough to bring the message this morning, and I'm believing God that he's gonna make a slam dunk of the Gospel." To that statement, the congregation broke into a murmur of laughs and giggles. It took all I had inside of me not to roll my eyes.

Reggie walked up to the podium, clutching his Bible, and shook the pastor's hand. "Thank you, Pastor Arnold, for this opportunity. Praise God for a chance to share His Word on this morning. Brothers and sisters, please turn in your Bibles to Romans 2:1."

I stood and looked on with Mama as she held her Bible between us and listened as Reggie read the verse. "I'll be reading from the New American Standard version for clarity. 'Therefore you have no excuse, every one of you who passes judgment, for in that which you judge another, you condemn yourself; for you who judge practice the same things'." He closed his Bible and then said. "Today I want to preach on the subject 'Be careful who you judge because it just might be you.' You may be seated."

"Amen," I said a little too loudly as I took my seat.

Reggie preached with passion and heart as he taught us the Biblical principal of  "Judge not lest ye be judged." It was a subject that really hit home with me. While he didn't posses the presence of T.D. Jakes or the charisma of Creflo Dollar (Yes, I knew who they were. I wasn't a total heathen), he had a good knowledge of the Bible and an obvious love for God and God's people. I was both impressed and shocked with his ability to engage the congregation as they sang a chorus of "amens" throughout his sermon. Instead of being bored to tears as I'd expected, I was actually interested in what he had to say and kept my eyes and ears locked on him.

Once service had ended, I stood beside Mama and smiled awkwardly as she hugged the fellow worshipers and said her goodbyes. By the time she was done and was poised to leave the sanctuary, Reggie approached us.

"Hello Sister Brooks, Bobbie Ann," he said with a nod to each of us.

"Hello, Reg— I mean, Reverend Darrough. Dat was a wonderful Word you brought dis mornin'," Mama said with a huge smile on her face.

He smiled at Mama and then looked at me. "Thank you. Um I'm gonna come and take care of your leak in a few minutes."

Mama nodded. "Okay, and you can stay and have dinner wit' us. I insist."

He laughed. "Yes ma'am. Just let me go and check on my mom and I'll be right on over."

"Okay, son. You tell yo' mama, Cassie, I said hi. I'mma send her a plate too."

"Yes ma'am." He smiled at me. "See y'all in a little bit."

I returned his smile and watched as he walked away. I was still smiling as Mama, Meka, Sharee, and I headed back across the yard to the house. I was definitely looking forward to seeing him again.

# TEN

### "Spoonful"

AFTER we'd made it back to the house, I quickly changed into a pair of jeans and an old Blues Festival t-shirt. I probably owned about a million of those t-shirts. I slipped on a pair of sneakers and walked into the kitchen where Mama, wearing a green knit robe over her church clothes, was standing at the counter with her back turned to the doorway. I stood there for a moment as the aroma of oven-barbecued chicken filled my nostrils.

Finally, I cleared my throat and spoke. "You need any help, Mama?"

She turned halfway around and eyed me. "Yeah, you can stir dis cornbread up for me and put it in da oven so I can git changed.

I nodded. "Okay, yes ma'am."

I took her place at the counter and stirred the yellow mixture until it was smooth and then poured it into the cast iron skillet. By the time she'd returned to the kitchen, wearing a blue blouse and matching pants, I'd already slid the pan onto the rack in the oven, above the pan of chicken.

I took a seat at the kitchen table as Mama checked on the greens, which were cooking in a huge pot on top of the stove. On the other side of the stove sat a long pan full of homemade macaroni and cheese which Mama had cooked before church that morning. She leaned over, opened the oven, and peaked at the food inside.

"Did I do it right?" I asked.

"Mm hmm. I'm surprised, doe. Didn't think you did much cookin' dees days," she said as she began to rinse off some dishes, her back to me.

I shook my head. "Never had much time, really."

"No time ta be a wife, huh? Any surprise he left cha?" she asked, her back still to me.

I sighed. *Here we go*, I thought. "Mama, my marriage wasn't a conventional one. It was more like a business partnership really. We understood each other's roles, and it worked for us."

She shook her head. "It worked up 'til now, huh? What happened ta make it stop workin'?"

I shrugged. "I really don't know. I thought we were doing okay."

She shut the water off and then turned around and looked me in the eye. "I'll tell you what happened, Bobbie Ann. What you thought was workin' wadnt workin at all, *ever*. It wadnt gone work because y'all didn't have God nowhere in dat relationship."

I looked down at my hands folded in my lap. "So that's it? If God was in it then it would've worked? It's that simple? That's how you and Daddy stayed together all those years?"

"Naw, you gotta have love, too. Love for each other, love for God. And appreciation, too. I appreciated yo' daddy for da man he was and for how he took care of us. Now you and Clyde didn't have dat. He used you, and you used him. Wadnt no love there far as I can tell."

"I did love him, though. I really did."

She shook her head. "You needed him ta take care uh you and dat's yo' daddy's fault. He was a good man, but he never let you stand on yo' own. Need ain't love, Bobbie Ann."

I knew she was right, but I really didn't want to hear it. I sat quietly for a moment and then changed the subject.

"How long Reggie been preaching?" I asked.

She sat down across from me at the table, the dish rag balled up in her hand. "Just since he been back home. Cassie say he got real close to da Lord cause uh da divorce, and dat's when he felt da callin'."

"So, they're already divorced?"

Mama nodded. "Mm hmm. It's a shame how dat woman did Reggie. He a real good man."

I leaned forward and asked, "What'd she do?"

She shook her head. "Cheated on him. Do you know dat girl had two kids befoe' he married her? Reggie treated dem kids like they was his own, and she did him like dat. Now she won't even let him have nothin' ta do wit em." That explained why he was so "hush

hush" about the kids.

"Didn't they have one child together, though?"

"It ain't his."

"What?!" I said, my eyes bucked.

"Yeah, had a little boy, named him Cassius, after Cassie. Turns out he wadnt none of Reggie's. She said it belonged ta one uh Reggie's teammates, and dat turned out ta be a lie, too. Don't know who da baby's daddy is. He was so hurt about it all, he jus' fell apart. Quit da team and came home to see 'bout Cassie, he say, but I think he needed her comfort too. Been here six months now."

"Wow, I'd have never guessed. Who would cheat on a man like Reggie?"

"A fool who don't see what a good man he is."

"Yeah, a total and complete fool," I agreed.

"Who's a fool?" It was Reggie who had joined our conversation. He was standing in the kitchen doorway.

I smiled and wondered how long he'd been standing there. "Uh, how'd you get in?" I asked, ignoring his question.

He returned my smile. "The girls let me in through the den."

"Oh," was my only answer.

"How's Cassie doin'?" Mama asked.

"She's alright. Her nurse is with her now. She wishes she could've been at church, though."

Mama nodded. "Well, I'mma call her and tell her 'bout dat wonderful sermon." She turned to me. "Bobbie Ann, you watch da food. Reggie, you know where da washer is." She stood to leave.

"Yes ma'am," Reggie said as Mama left the kitchen. He turned to me and said, "She's still the boss around here, huh?"

I nodded. "Definitely, and she rules with an iron fist. You'd better get to work."

He laughed. "Yeah, see you in a little bit."

♫♫♫

Nearly an hour later, I stepped out the back door and across the back yard to the shed to get Reggie for dinner. I walked into the shed to find him in the process of pushing the machine back against the wall. The muscles in his arms bulged as he moved against the machine.

"Um, all fixed?" I asked.

He nodded as he wiped his hands on his jeans. "Yeah, I think so. I ran it through a couple of cycles and no leaks."

"Great. Well, you're done just in time for dinner."

He smiled. "Good, because I'm starving." He rubbed his stomach.

I laughed. "Okay, come on."

Reggie followed me across the yard and into the house. I had to resist the desire to twist my hips a little as I walked. He made me want to flirt with him. Hell, he made me want to do a lot of things with him. At that point, if Reggie had given me the signal, I would've been all over that fine body of his. I had to remind myself that he was a preacher. He wouldn't be caught dead with a sinner like me, especially with our past between us.

We walked into the tiny dining room, adjacent to the kitchen, to find Mama and the girls already seated. The only free seats at the table were side by side. We quietly sat down next to each other.

"Reggie, would you bless da food?" Mama asked.

"Um, yes ma'am," he said. We all bowed our heads and closed our eyes as he prayed. "Heavenly Father, first giving thanks for all good and perfect things come from you. Thank you, Father, for the food that has been prepared and bless it to nourish our bodies. It's in Jesus' name we pray, Amen."

"Amen," we all said in agreement.

We all immediately piled our plates high and began to eat. No, I couldn't get along with my mama, but that woman could cook! If I kept eating like this, my hips were going to spread as wide as the house.

"My goodness, Ms. Mae, this is some good food!" Reggie said, echoing my thoughts.

Mama smiled. "Thank you, Reggie."

"Yeah, it's delicious, Mama," I added.

Without looking up from her plate she said, "Well, you can cook tomorrow. 'Bout time you learned. I'll tell you what ta do and you can have dinner ready befoe' me and da girls get home." No "thank you" for me.

"Well, Mama that'll be hard. Remember I've got that appointment tomorrow." It was my first appointment with the therapist. "Oh yeah, and I'll need to drive my truck."

"No ma'am," she answered, looking me dead in the eye.

I hated to get into an argument with company present, but she was really being unreasonable. "But it's in Arkadelphia. That's more than an hour away. I can't walk that far, Mama."

Mama frowned. "I know dat." She turned to Reggie. "You busy tomorrow, Reggie?"

Reggie looked up from his plate. "Um, no ma'am."

Well you think you could drive Bobbie Ann ta her appointment tomorrow?"

"Uh, yes ma'am. No problem."

Mama looked at me. "What time is yo' appointment?"

I couldn't believe her. She was going to have Reggie drive me to see a shrink? How embarrassing!

I looked down at the table and said, "Eleven."

She looked at Reggie. "Reggie, can you pick her up 'round nine-thirty?"

He nodded. "Yes ma'am."

She returned her gaze to me. "Then it's settled, and you don't need ta drive."

I stared down at the table and sighed. "Yes, ma'am."

# ELEVEN

## "Still Called the Blues"

AT 9:30 A.M. on the dot, I heard a knock at the den door. I was fully dressed, but barefoot with a scarf still covering my hair, when I opened the door and let Reggie in.

"Good morning," he said with a smile. He was dressed in a pair of brown cargo pants and a navy blue polo shirt. A cross on a gold chain hung around his neck.

"Good morning. Sorry I'm running late. Be ready in a few minutes." I said and then dashed back into the bedroom as Reggie took a seat on the sofa.

"Alright," was his reply. Reggie just had a laid back, easy nature about him at all times.

I quickly applied my make-up, snatched the scarf off my head, and picked my hair out. I slipped on a pair of gold heels that complimented my gold t-shirt and dark skinny jeans. I inspected myself in the short dresser mirror, grabbed my jacket and purse, and then headed back into the den.

"Okay, I'm ready," I announced.

Reggie looked up at me. "Wow, that was quick. You look amazing."

I blushed like a 14-year-old being complimented by her crush. "Um, thanks."

We left the house, and I closed and locked the door behind us, then climbed into Reggie's huge SUV.

"It's not luxury like yours but it'll do, huh?" Reggie asked as he climbed into the driver's seat.

I shook my head. "You're kidding, right? This is a really nice truck, Reg."

"Well, thanks, Ms. Brooks. I just know a star like you is used to luxury, you know?"

"My life has not been nearly as luxurious as you might think, Mr. Darrough," I scoffed.

Reggie shrugged his shoulders and started the truck. We rode mostly in silence, save the gospel music that was softly playing on the truck's radio. About thirty miles into the ride, I began the conversation.

"So I guess you know I'm gonna see a shrink today," I said.

Reggie kept his eyes glued to the road and shook his head. "No, I didn't, actually."

"Yeah, well the doctor in Dallas suggested I seek therapy. I doubt it'll help anything. I think I'm a hopeless case." I rolled my eyes for dramatic effect.

"Well, like anything else, you'll get out of it what you put into it, right?"

I shrugged my shoulders. "Well anyway, that's where I'm going." I looked out of the window and drummed my fingers on my thigh then added, "Did you know I was in the hospital back in Dallas? Before Mama brought me back home against my will?"

Reggie cleared his throat. "Um, Bobbie, you don't have to tell me any of this if you—"

"No," I interrupted. "It's alright. I mean you're driving me a long ways. You should at least know why. It's only fair."

He glanced at me and nodded. "Okay."

"I was in the hospital for alcohol poisoning," I said matter-of-factly.

Reggie didn't reply but kept his eyes on the road.

I looked down at my hands in my lap. "I mean, how messed up is that? Usually someone poisons someone else, but I managed to poison myself and with liquor, no less. I think I tried to drink myself to death."

Reggie flashed me a concerned look. "You *think*?" He asked.

I looked up at him. "Yeah, well I don't exactly know what I was doing. I guess I don't know much of anything anymore. I got those divorce papers and I just snapped. Drank up everything in the house that was fermented."

Reggie frowned. "Y'all hadn't discussed divorce before that?"

I shook my head and laughed bitterly. "Naw, his sorry ass just disappeared while I was on tour. Oh, excuse my French, Rev. Anyway, when I finally got home, his stuff was gone and the next thing I know I'm getting served with divorce papers." I paused and blinked back tears. "It's like he just threw me away. You know, like a piece of trash." *I feel like a piece of trash.*

"There were no signs that any of this was coming? I mean, I just don't know how anyone could do another person like that. Especially someone they love." Reggie queried.

I twisted my mouth and looked back out the window. "Yeah, I guess there were signs. We fought a lot, and he'd just disappear sometimes. I guess I just chose to ignore what was going on." I ran my fingers through my hair and sighed. "I suppose I thought that things would get better between us, but they didn't."

He nodded knowingly. "Yeah, I been there too."

"Um Reg? Mama told me about your divorce. I'm sorry."

He tightened his grip on the steering wheel. "Yeah, I am too."

"Um, she told me about the kids, too," I said softly.

Reggie was quiet and never took his eyes off the road.

I looked down at my hands and said, "I understand if you don't wanna talk about it."

Reggie cleared his throat again. "Not much to talk about. It hurt me, it really did. I wanted a family more than anything, but sometimes things just don't work out as planned. I dealt with it and moved on."

"It's that simple, huh? Just move on."

He glanced at me and shook his head. "Nothing's that simple but with God it's a lot less difficult. God brought me through. The only way I could've made it is with Him."

"Are you still angry with her?"

"Who, my wife?"

I nodded. "Yeah."

He shook his head. "Naw, I forgave her long ago. I mean, nothing's ever totally one person's fault. I worked a lot and was hardly ever home. Anyway, I believe that God made one woman for one man. We all have a God-designed mate. Obviously, she wasn't the one he made for me. If she was, we'd still be together."

"Yeah, I see what you mean."

For the remainder of the ride to Dr. Barlow's office, we were both quiet. As he pulled up to the large beige building, I felt a nervousness come over me. Reggie had parked and killed the engine, and I just sat there and stared at the glass doors which led into the office.

"Um, Bobbie it's 10:45," Reggie said.

"I know," I replied. I sat there a few more minutes and then opened the truck door. I stopped and looked over at Reggie. "You'll be here when I'm done?" I asked.

Reggie offered me a sweet smile and nodded his head. "I won't budge."

I returned his smile with a weak one of my own. "Okay."

I walked into the office, signed in, and waited for my name to be called. After only a few minutes seated in the waiting area between a burly, quiet Caucasian man and a friendly, elderly Caucasian woman, my name was finally called. I stood and walked over to the petite receptionist and listened as she instructed me on how to complete the intake forms. It had only been a few minutes since I'd returned the forms to her when she called my name again, signaling that it was now time for me to meet with Dr. Barlow.

Iva Barlow was a short brunette woman who probably wore a size six, but a four was not out of the question. She wore a navy blue blazer with matching slacks, a baby blue blouse, and sensible black shoes. Her bone straight hair fell to her shoulders and other than the red lipstick on her ultra thin lips, she wore no make-up.

As I entered the room, decorated in warm earth tones, Dr. Barlow greeted me with a wide smile and a firm handshake. I took a seat in a comfortable brown leather chair as Dr. Barlow sat directly across from me in a matching chair. She adjusted her glasses on her face and then began her version of an ice-breaker.

"I'm Dr. Barlow, but everyone calls me I.B. I've been a practicing psychologist for ten years. I'm married, and we're the proud parents of two fat cats, Muriel and Bill. I love major league baseball. But more than anything, I love helping others." She paused to smile at me again. "Tell me about you."

I took a deep breath and then released it. I clasped my hands in my lap and twisted my mouth as I began to speak. "Um, my name is Bobbie Brooks, but I guess you know that. Anyway, most people that know me well call me Bobbie Ann. Well, actually, my full name is Bobbie BluAnn Brooks. That's how it is on my birth certificate, really. And dear Lord, I'm rambling. I'm sorry. I'm so nervous." I placed my right hand on my forehead and closed my eyes.

Dr. Barlow offered me a smile and said, "Which would you prefer

I called you?"

I stared at the floor and then fixed my eyes on her shoes. They were black leather Mary Janes. "Um, Bobbie is fine."

"Okay Bobbie, I like to start my sessions out by allowing my clients a moment of silent meditation. You can pray or take deep breaths; whatever you need to do to get yourself centered and ready to work.

I looked up at her. "Um, okay."

I closed my eyes for a moment and tried to clear my thoughts. After a minute or so, I actually felt a lot calmer. I opened my eyes and looked across at Dr. Barlow, who was still smiling.

"Bobbie, why do you think you're here today?" she asked.

I cleared my throat and shrugged. "I guess I have a drinking problem."

She nodded. "Okay, what do you mean by 'drinking problem'?" She made quotation marks in the air with her fingers.

I shifted my eyes to a landscape painting hanging on the wall. "I mean, I drink too much sometimes. That's why I was in the hospital."

She clasped her hands in her lap. "Do you always drink that much? Enough to go to the hospital?" She asked.

I shook my head. "No. I drank a lot before, but I guess those were special circumstances."

"How so?"

"Um well, this last time I'd just been served with divorce papers, and I guess I was kinda upset about it." I shifted in my seat.

She nodded. "I see. What triggered the drinking before that?"

"Um, if I was on the road, before a show, I drank. Oh yeah, by the way, I'm a singer."

"Okay, so you drank before a show, and…"

"Well during the shows also, and when I'm upset or frustrated sometimes I drink. But it's not like I'm an alcoholic. I mean, I don't drink *all the time*."

"Okay." She stood and walked across the room, gathered some pamphlets from a bookshelf and then reclaimed her seat. "Bobbie, what do you think is the definition of an alcoholic?"

I shrugged. "Someone who's got to have it all the time. Someone who *needs* it." I looked up at her.

"And you don't need it?"

I shook my head. What was she getting at? "No, I don't. I haven't had a drink since the day I left the hospital.

"Have you wanted to drink?"

I sat and thought for a moment. Truthfully, I had wanted to drink since the moment I set foot back in Willisville. Maybe the memories were too much for me.

"Um, yeah. I guess so," I answered.

She nodded slowly. "And what triggered the desire to drink?"

"I guess you could say it was stress, bad feelings."

"Okay, Bobbie, can I give you a definition of alcoholism?"

I nodded. "Well, sure."

"Alcoholism is one's dependence on alcohol."

I raised my eyebrows. "Okay." I really didn't know what she was getting at.

"Dependence is defined as a reliance on something or someone for help or support."

I frowned. "So you think that—"

She shook her head as she interrupted me. "I don't think anything Bobbie. Based on that definition, what do *you* think?

"Based on what you said, I guess I could have a problem with alcohol," I said softly.

"Okay," was her only reply.

I leaned forward in my seat. "Look, I *can't* be an alcoholic. I'm not anything like the alcoholics I've seen and known. I'm not messed up like them. I've seen people that drink all the time. They'll be falling down drunk in the middle of the day. That's not me."

"Did you know that there are stages of alcoholism?"

I rolled my eyes. "Well no, you're the expert, right?" She was beginning to get on my nerves.

"Bobbie, I know the thought of you having a problem like this is upsetting to you, but I really am here to help you."

I closed my eyes and nodded.

Dr. Barlow continued by explaining the stages of alcoholism. "There's early, middle, and end. Now, the alcoholics you referred to are undoubtedly in the end stage. From what you've told me about yourself, you might be somewhere in between the early and middle stages. The thing is, even in the earlier stages of alcoholism, the drinking can lead to reckless behaviors like drunk driving, drug use, anonymous sex, and so on."

I flinched. She'd been reading my mail. I opened my eyes and looked at her. "Well, if I'm an alcoholic, shouldn't I be going to AA instead of here?" I asked, feeling frustrated

She nodded. "Actually, I recommend both. I believe attending weekly AA meetings would be of a great benefit to you, but one-on-one therapy will be beneficial as well."

I sighed. "Whatever you think is best."

"Bobbie, this is about you and you taking control of your life. You know, alcoholism can be directly connected to control issues. When some people feel like they've lost control of something important, they use alcohol to dull or even mask the painful emotions. Do you believe that you have control issues?"

"Well, yeah I do." Lack of control would have been a better way of putting it. I looked up at Dr. Barlow. "Okay, I think that your plan sounds good. AA and therapy."

She nodded. "Alright, I wanna give you some information." She handed me the pamphlets that she'd been holding in her lap. "These will give you some good information on alcoholism and Alcoholics Anonymous, including information about local meeting times and places."

I took the information from her and moments later, she walked me out into the waiting area. "See you in two weeks," she said.

I nodded in agreement. "Okay."

I was so preoccupied with what we'd discussed that I didn't even notice Reggie sitting in the waiting area. I had already opened the glass doors which led outside to the parking lot when I felt a hand on my shoulder.

I turned around to see Reggie giving me a concerned look. "Bobbie, you okay? You breezed right by me back there."

I looked up at him with tears forming in my eyes. "No, I'm not okay. Evidently, I'm an alcoholic. Damn!" I said, my voice breaking.

Reggie pulled me into his arms. I buried my face in his chest and cried.

♫♫♫

We stopped at a local Mexican restaurant for lunch, but realizing that I was alcoholic had ruined my appetite. I sat across from Reggie and picked at the food on my plate.

"You don't like the food?" Reggie asked between bites of his huge burrito.

I shrugged and without looking up from my plate said, "Not hungry."

"Superstar, I know you're upset, but you can beat this thing with God's help. I know it."

"Well Reg, I don't think God'll be too eager help me," I scoffed.

Reggie gave me a confused look. "Why would you say that? You're his child just like I am. He loves you."

I laughed resentfully. "Well, let's see. My husband and manager left me and then he stole all of my money from me. So I'm basically penniless now. I don't even know how to take care of my own business affairs because I've never had to. I'm stuck in a house with a mother who hates me and to top it all off, I just realized that I'm a freakin' alcoholic. You know, I don't even have a divorce lawyer. Hell, I can't afford one, not even a bad one. So Clyde'll probably take everything I've worked for all these years." I slumped back into my chair. "Sound like a child of God to you?"

"It sounds like God's opportunity to show you that you're his child."

I shook my head. "I can't see it, Reverend Reggie."

Reggie leaned forward and looked me in the eye. "Let me help you, Bobbie. You can use my divorce lawyer. I'll pay for it."

I sat up straight. "No, Reggie. I can't let you do that. I just can't."

"Yeah, you can. Look, you can pay me back if you want. You know, whenever you get your finances straightened out."

I closed my eyes and shook my head. I didn't want to accept his offer, but what choice did I have? If I didn't get a lawyer and soon, Clyde would take everything from me.

I sighed and then said, "Okay, but I'm gonna pay you back. I promise."

Reggie smiled. "Okay, no rush. You'll love Shelly. She's a terrific lawyer. Her office is in Little Rock."

"You have a female lawyer?"

"I have a *good* lawyer. One of the best. I'll set everything up."

"Um thanks, Reg. I really appreciate it." I paused and then said, "Um, I have these AA meetings to attend and they're at night, here in Arkadelphia and I'd hate for Mama to have to drive me and—"

Reggie raised his hand. "Say no more. I've got plenty of time on my hands. I'll take you wherever you need to go whenever you need to be there. It's no problem at all."

I smiled. "Thanks Reggie, but you may get tired of me and my messed up life."

He returned my smile. "Never that, Superstar."

I managed to relocate my appetite, finished my meal, and soon afterwards, we left for Willisville.

# TWELVE

## "The Truth Will Set You Free"

TUESDAY and Wednesday passed without incident, and I found myself quickly falling into a regular routine. Up at six, breakfast with Mama and the girls, clean the kitchen and make my bed, bathe, dress, write, and try to cook dinner per Mama's instructions. It was the hours during the day when I was all alone that I found difficult to cope with. It was during the times of complete quiet and stillness that my mind would wander into thoughts of Clyde, the road, and the stage. It was also those times when the desire to drink was at its greatest point. I missed my old life. It wasn't perfect, but it was all I knew.

More than anything, I missed my sweet daddy, and I wished that I could talk to him. There were so many reminders of him at home that I could almost feel him. So, on Tuesday morning, I decided to get as close to him as I could. After I'd completed my morning chores, I slipped on a pair of jeans, a pink t-shirt, and a pair of sneakers, and then set out to walk the two miles to St. Peter's cemetery, where my father was buried.

I shoved my hands into the pockets of my jeans and carelessly kicked at a few loose rocks as I made my way down the red clay driveway. I glanced over at the church and noticed Reggie's truck parked on the side near the door which led into the kitchen. *Wonder what he's up to?* I thought.

I turned my attention back to the road ahead of me. I walked from the driveway onto the short gravel road that led from my mother's house out to the main road. The main road snaked through the small community of fewer than 200 people. Five minutes later, I was well on my way to the cemetery. I passed several small houses, some older, some newer. To my left, a grove of pine trees, and to my right, a small trailer home complete with chicken coop and pig pen. I smiled to myself. Talk about a fish out of water. Up until this point, the past several years of my life had consisted of hotel rooms, stages in dark clubs, concerts and blues fests, shopping sprees, room service, and automatic everything. I'd almost forgotten that chickens lived in coops and pigs in pens.

I continued what I had at first believed would be an easy journey and quickly realized just how out of shape I was. It seemed that I had grossly overestimated my level of physical fitness. I stopped and leaned against a fire engine red mailbox, and tried to catch my breath. The name on the box read Miller. No one I knew of. I bent over and placed my hands on my knees as I eyed the road ahead of me.

Finally, I took a deep breath and then stepped back onto the road.

After about five minutes, the dirt road that led directly to the cemetery came into view. I breathed a sigh of relief and continued to walk. Moments later I could hear the soft whir of a vehicle's engine behind me. Without looking back, I moved off the road and onto the grassy shoulder, continuing to walk. The car didn't speed up but continued to creep along the road behind me. *Who is this idiot? I* wondered. *And what do they want me to do?* I shook my head and continued to walk until finally, the stupidity of what was happening overcame me.

Frowning, I spun on my heels, ready to see what the driver's problem was.

"What's wrong with you?!" I yelled, before realizing that it was Reggie who was driving slowly behind me.

He stopped his vehicle and then jumped out of the driver's seat, laughing loudly. "Did I scare you?"

I continued to frown. I was not amused. "No, actually you annoyed me. What were you doing?"

He shrugged. "Just messing with you. I'm sorry," he said softly.

I rolled my eyes and turned to head back towards the cemetery.

"Um, where you headed? Need a ride?" Reggie asked, stopping me in my tracks.

Well I *was* tired, but nevertheless, I shook my head and said, "I'm fine."

He smiled and his eyes sparkled. I placed my hand on my chest. He was just so beautiful.

"Aw, now. Come on, I said I was sorry," he said. He moved so close to me that I could smell his cologne in the open air. "Where you going, Superstar? Let me, uh, be your chauffeur," He said barely above a whisper.

I looked up at him and for a brief moment was unable to answer him. But I gathered my senses and softly said, "Um, the cemetery."

He looked down at me. "Hop in. I'm at your service."

I nodded absently as he walked over to the vehicle and opened the passenger door. He was wearing gray sweat pants, and a black t-shirt. A black baseball cap covered his curly hair. I watched his 6'7" frame as he walked in front of me and smiled. He looked like he was ready to hit the basketball court at any moment.

I climbed into the black leather seat and watched as he closed my door and then walked around the front of the vehicle and climbed in beside me.

"Alright, Superstar. Let's go," he said as he turned the key in the ignition and put the vehicle in gear.

"I saw your truck parked at the church earlier. What were you doing in there?" I asked as I stared at his huge hands on the steering wheel.

"Cleaning up," he answered without taking his eyes off the road.

"Man, Reggie. You're a jack of all trades, huh? You preach, fix, clean, *and* play basketball. What *don't* you do?"

He grinned and glanced at me. "Not much."

I smiled. "I believe you."

I stared out the window and then said, "Hey, I was wondering

Why'd you decide to play overseas instead of in the US? I know some NBA teams must've wanted you."

He looked at me with his eyebrows raised. "You been wondering about me huh? Had me on your mind? I'm honored, Ms. Brooks."

I rolled my eyes. "Just answer the question, Darrough."

He chuckled and said, "Well, one of my college coaches advised me to check into playing in the European leagues. I researched it and found that those teams pay really good and give some pretty good perks, too. Plus, just like here, I've had great-paying endorsements, and I got to literally travel the world. I played for an Italian team, lived in Milan. I really enjoyed it."

"Enjoyed?" I asked. "Have you quit playing for good?"

He shrugged. "I don't know. I guess my heart's not really in it right now. I always said I wouldn't mind coaching one day though, but who knows what the future will bring."

I nodded. "Yeah, who knows?" I certainly never thought it would bring me back to Willisville.

"You ever been overseas, Bobbie?"

"Yeah, I've done a few shows in Europe. Blues is pretty popular over there. I've performed in England, Holland, even Germany."

"You should've looked me up. I would've loved to catch one of your shows."

I looked out the window and said, "Yeah, I thought about it, but I guess I figured you wouldn't be interested in seeing me."

"Well, you thought wrong," he said softly.

A few minutes later, we'd arrived at the cemetery. It was old but well kept and although I hadn't been there in years, I knew exactly where my daddy was buried. By the time Reggie made it to the passenger side, I'd already swung the door open.

"Dang, Superstar. You know, chivalry ain't dead *everywhere*. I was gonna open that for you," he said.

I gave him a sheepish look. "Sorry, I guess I'm not used to it." Well, actually, I wasn't used to chivalry at all and anywhere.

He shook his head as he took my hand and helped me out of the truck. "Your husband's a loser," he said under his breath.

"Who you telling?" I said.

We walked through the open gate and onto the uneven ground of the cemetery. I headed directly to the southwest corner where my dad was buried alongside his mother and father. Once I reached his grave, I stood before the gray headstone and read it as if I'd never seen it before. "Earl James Brooks, Sr. Adoring husband and loving father. Born April 2, 1954. Died December 30, 2004." The other side of the stone, reserved for my mother, was blank. Cancer had taken my father at an early age and the pain I felt was just as deep as it had been the day he died.

A single tear rolled down my cheek as I stood before my father's final resting place. I wiped it away and then turned to Reggie, who stood directly behind me. "Um, can you give me a few minutes alone?"

He placed his hand on my shoulder. "Sure. I'm gonna go and see my grandma's grave. I won't be far if you need me."

I nodded. "Okay."

Reggie walked away, and I sat on my father's grave and faced the stone.

"Daddy, it's me. I've been missing you a lot lately. A bunch of stuff's been going on in my life, and my head's really jumbled up. I wish you were here. I wish you could help me." The tears began to pour from my eyes, and I lowered my head as I sobbed.

A minute or so later, I wiped my eyes, took a deep breath, and continued to speak. "Um, Clyde left me and stole all my money. I've been sick and in the hospital from drinking too much. I drink a lot sometimes Daddy. I'm glad you're not here to see what a mess I've made of my life." I turned to see Reggie standing at the opposite end of the cemetery.

I turned back to my father's grave. "I'm staying with Mama and the girls right now. Things with Mama are the same…"

I continued to talk until I thought I'd covered everything. Then I remembered to mention Reggie.

"Reggie's back here, too. He's been real nice to me. I think I still care about him, and I kinda wish we could get back together. But I know we can't. There's something that happened back when we were together before that I never told him about. If he knew he'd never forgive me."

The sound of leaves crunching behind me silenced me. I turned around and looked up at Reggie, hoping that he hadn't heard me. Judging from the wide smile he gave me, I guessed that he hadn't.

"You ready, Superstar? You still got that meeting tonight, right?" He asked referring to my first AA meeting.

I nodded as he offered me a hand up off of the ground. "Yeah, I do."

He helped me to my feet and then said. "Well, let me get you back home so you can rest up for tonight."

I smiled. "Okay and thank you, Reggie. For everything."

"My pleasure, Bobbie Ann," he said as he took my hand and led me to his truck.

♫♫♫

As I walked into the Fellowship Hall of the Arkadelphia Assembly of God Church, I was a ball of nerves. Reggie walked me into the building and promised he'd only be a phone call away if I needed him. Usually, the meetings were closed to the general public.

After he left, I stood at the back of the room and surveyed my surroundings. There was a podium and microphone situated in front of a few rows of folding chairs arranged in two even sections. At the back of the room there was a folding table with iron legs and a thick white plastic top. Behind the table stood a gray-haired, worn-faced white man who was serving Styrofoam cups of coffee or water.

There were about fifteen people in attendance, including me. Most of them were older white men, or at least they looked older. There was one other woman in the room. She was short and wide with long black hair. I thought that she was probably Hispanic. She looked older as well but was still really pretty. *I don't belong here.* I thought. *I'm nothing like these people.* Their clothes were faded and wrinkled, their shoes were run-over, and their bodies looked worn. These people were *real* alcoholics. I was definitely not in the category with them.

I turned to leave but before I could take one step towards the door, I felt a hand on my shoulder. I jumped and then turned around and found myself face to face with the coffee man.

"Sorry I startled you, but I know that look," he said with a warm smile and a soothing voice. "Everyone has that look their first meeting. I'm Lee Faust. You must be Bobbie." He held his hand out.

I nodded and grasped his hand. "Um, yes I am."

"I'm the program coordinator and the pastor of this church *and* an alcoholic."

My eyes widened. "Oh, um…"

"And you think that you don't belong here, right?"

I shifted my eyes from his face, feeling a little guilty. "Well, I…"

"How about this? Give it a chance, one meeting. And if you still feel the same afterwards, you never have to come back."

I dropped my eyes. "Okay, I guess."

He smiled brightly. "You want some coffee? Water, maybe?"

I smiled weakly. "Water's fine."

"Alright! Well step right over here, and I'll get you all fixed up."

I followed him over to the table and smiled as he handed me a Styrofoam cup of water.

"Now, you can sit anywhere you like," he said with a bright smile on his face. His genuine friendliness put me at ease.

I smiled and nodded. "Okay, thanks."

A few minutes later, I took a seat on the third row to the left of the podium and bowed my head as Rev. Faust prayed. When he was finished, it was introduction time. By then five or six more people had trickled into the room and taken their seats, including a black couple who sat a few rows behind me. I sat quietly as everyone around me stood and gave their first names, ending their introductions with, "and I'm an alcoholic."

When they were finished, everyone applauded and Rev. Faust, or Lee as he preferred to be called, said, "I'm glad you all could make it tonight. God bless you!" He smiled and then continued to speak. "Guys, we have a new person here with us tonight, and I want you to make her feel real welcome." He turned his gaze to me and nodded.

I stood reluctantly and said, "Um, I'm Bobbie and um, I'm an alcoholic." It almost sounded like a question because, I guess, I still wasn't really sure if I *was* one.

My statement was met with a chorus of "Great to meet you, Bobbie." I smiled nervously and then reclaimed my seat.

Lee spoke into the mic again. "Well Bobbie, we're up to step five tonight, but I'll get you some information on all twelve steps.

I nodded.

"Okay folks, what is step five?" Lee asked.

The crowd answered in unison. "We've admitted to God, to ourselves, and to another human being, the exact nature of our wrongs."

Lee nodded. "That's right, and tonight Don wants to share his story with us. It kinda ties into step five. Don."

Lee left the podium and to my surprise, the lone black man in the room took the floor. He cleared his throat and tensely rubbed his hand across his bald head, which glistened with sweat. Dressed in a blue jean suit and beige dress shirt, he was obviously nervous.

"Um, I'm Don and I'm an alcoholic."

The crowd replied with, "Welcome, Don."

"Um, thanks. A lot of you already know me and some don't. That's my wife Velma back there." He nodded to his wife who stood and smiled at the small crowd.

Don carried on with his speech. "Um, I'm originally from Prescott. Born and raised there. I was pretty smart, got a scholarship to college."

He scratched his forehead and continued. "I, uh, got a degree in accounting and finance. I was always real good with numbers, and I went on to get an MBA. Um about eight years ago, I guess you can say that I had it all. A really good job with an accounting firm in Memphis, a nice house, and by then I'd married my wife, Velma. We'd known each other since high school, and we'd finally made it official. Everything was going good."

Don paused and cleared his throat. "Then I started going out with the guys from the office after work. You know, a drink here or there. No big deal, just a little fun. Even business dinners or parties included a bar. It just became a way of life to drink in just about every situation. You almost feel obligated to drink. You know, so you can fit in. As time went on, I started getting larger and more important accounts, and the pressure started getting to me. I went from casual drinking to habitual drinking. I'd drink to mask my anxiety and stress. The pressures of life just started weighing me down. I was so afraid of disappointing my family, everyone.

"I worked insane hours and barely spent any time with Velma. She was pregnant by then with our first child, and I wasn't any support to her. I'd hit the bar every night after work and drank nearly all weekend long at home. My work suffered and so did my family. By the time Velma had our daughter, I was almost unbearable to live with.

"I ended up losing my job and my drinking got worse. Me and Velma argued all the time. I made her life miserable. Well, one night after we had a big blowout, I left the house and went to my favorite place, the liquor store. I sat in my car in the parking lot of that liquor store and drank until everything I'd bought was empty and then I drove home. I was obviously drunk and I was driving too fast and there was an accident." Don paused.

He rubbed his eyes, and then began to speak again. "Um, I ran into a car, a family. I...I was the only survivor." Don broke down at that point.

I looked back at his wife who was also in tears. I felt a few tears begin to well up in my eyes as well. Lee walked over to Don and patted his shoulder then whispered something in his ear.

Don nodded and then continued to speak. "Um, they were young. The husband, Shawn, was 26. The wife, Kelly, was 25. The kids, Braylyn and Brooklyn, were five and four. And I killed them all. I went to jail, mandatory treatment, lost my house, and Velma left me.

I came back to Arkansas a failure. I had to move back in with my mom. I'd hit rock bottom."

*Tell me about it*, I thought.

I returned my attention to Don as he continued to speak. "I'd been back a few months and was still in a really bad place when I started coming to these meetings. Lee was a Godsend. We got to step five, and I knew the only way I could get better was to apologize and ask everyone for forgiveness. So I did. I started off with God, who was gracious to forgive me. Then I called the parents of the wife and husband that were killed in the accident, and they listened to me. I don't know if they'll ever forgive me, but at least they listened.

"But the hardest task of all was calling Velma. I knew I'd disappointed her in so many ways, but she forgave me right away. Our little girl, Asia, she's seven now, and she's smart and happy and beautiful. We have a son, too now. I'm working here at the church, now and things are good. I thank Lee, Velma, and most of all, God, for forgiving me and giving me another chance."

Don received a standing ovation.

When the meeting was over, I walked out onto the parking lot to find Reggie leaning against the hood of his truck with his arms folded across his chest, waiting for me. I smiled and walked towards the vehicle where he, of course, opened my door for me. We rode back to Willisville underneath a star-filled sky in peaceful silence.

Reggie didn't ask about the meeting. It was as if he sensed that I really didn't want to discuss it. Once we'd reached my mom's house, he parked in the driveway and walked me to the door.

"Goodnight, Superstar," he said as he leaned over and kissed me on the forehead.

I smiled up at him. "Goodnight, Reggie. And thank you."

I went inside the house and before long, settled into bed. I fell into a troubled sleep as the thought kept running through my mind that the only person I'd ever really wronged in my life was Reggie, but how could I tell him?

# THIRTEEN

## "You Can't Lose What You Ain't Never Had"

THE rest of the week raced right on by. Funny how time flies when you're not having fun. Even funnier the things you can get used to no matter how long you've been away from them. But funniest is how some things just never change.

I watched day after day as Mama got up at the crack of dawn, got dressed for work, cooked breakfast, dropped the girls off at the bus stop, and then drove off to work, herself. In all those years, Mama hadn't changed a bit. From the tight bun on her head to the wire-rimmed glasses and even to that old Buick, nothing had changed. Nothing, not even her contempt for me.

I lived in that house with her but felt like an outsider. I really wished that I could discuss my therapy or the AA meeting with her, but when I tried, she always cut me off. It was as if it disinterested her to hear about me or my life. Maybe she interpreted it as whining. She was a strong, tough woman and had always had a low tolerance for crying and whining. I became resigned to the fact that we'd never be close, and I would just have to accept that fact just as I always had. I told myself that as soon as my mind was clear and my affairs were in order, I'd move back home to Dallas and hopefully hit the studio in full force. I missed my old life, no matter how dysfunctional it might have been.

Monday morning, just after Mama and the girls left, I took a quick bath and dressed for my appointment with Attorney Shelly Mixon. I arrived early and as Reggie and I waited in her modestly decorated outer office, I wondered about his divorce. I knew it had been painful for him. He still had a hard time talking about it. I wondered how long it took someone to heal from something as devastating as an unwanted divorce.

"Ms. Brooks?" The short, compact receptionist inquired.

"Yes," I answered, snapping out of thoughts.

"Ms. Mixon will see you now."

I nodded and looked at Reggie.

He smiled. "It's okay, go ahead. I'll be right here."

"Okay," I said, but I didn't believe it was okay. For a woman who'd never had much control of her own life, I was sure being forced into doing a lot of things independently.

I stood and smoothed the front of my chocolate brown pencil skirt. I adjusted the collar of my gold blouse and hung my purse on my shoulder as I walked into Ms. Mixon's office. It was a sleekly decorated space with cream-colored walls and deep brown carpet. On the wall hung certificates from Howard University and Berkeley Law.

Shelly Mixon was a tall, thin woman who looked to be in her early forties. She possessed keen European features and flowing, wavy, black hair. She wore white slacks, a black blouse, and black and white checkered heels. Her rectangular wire-rimmed glasses were balanced on the tip of her long nose. At first sight, Ms. Mixon appeared to be Hispanic or maybe even Italian, but as soon as she opened her mouth, it was clear that she was a black woman.

She extended her hand to me as I walked over to her huge mahogany desk. "Ms. Brooks? Shelly Mixon. It's good to meet you. Mr. Darrough has told me a lot about you."

"Um, good to meet you, too," I said as I gripped her hand. Her handshake was firm; a hint to her assertive confidence.

She nodded towards a brown leather wing-backed chair situated in front of her desk and said, "Have a seat."

I quickly sat down, crossed my legs, and placed my purse in my lap.

"Ms. Brooks, you'll find that I'm a very straight-forward person. I'm a businesswoman, and my time is very precious to me." She paused and leaned forward, placing her perfectly manicured hands on her desk. "So I need to know if there is any chance that you and your husband will reconcile." She looked me straight in the eye, awaiting my answer.

I was a little taken aback by her introductory remarks. "Straight-forward" was a gross understatement. "Um, I don't even know where my husband is living, and I haven't heard from him in weeks so, no."

She raised her eyebrows. "You're sure about that? I'm pretty expensive, and I'd hate to waste Mr. Darrough's money. Maybe you could find him and the two of you could work things out."

I shook my head. "There's no way we're getting back together. No way at all."

She smiled. "Good. Now that that's clear, let me tell you a little about me. I'm a good lawyer, a damn good one. And I can play hard ball with the best of them. I don't pull punches, and I fight feverishly for my clients. There's nothing that I'm unwilling to do, within the letter of the law, of course, to ensure the best possible outcome for my clients. But you understand that I must have your full cooperation."

I nodded. I was feeling a little too intimidated to speak.

"I'm licensed in three states, including Texas, and I am very familiar with divorce law," she said.

I nodded again. "Okay."

"Ms. Brooks, tell me why you and your husband are ending your marriage."

"Um, I gave you the papers, right?"

"Yes, but I'd like for you to tell me in your own words."

I filled her in on everything from our financial arrangements to his disappearance in Chicago, to my hospitalization. Once I was finished she twisted her mouth and stared at me for a moment.

Then she flipped her hair behind her shoulder and shifted in her seat. "Well, Ms. Brooks, let me give you the good news first."

I placed my hand on my knee to stop the nervous tapping of

my foot, not wanting to display any signs of weakness. But then again, the story I'd just told her screamed "weak!"

"Alright," I said evenly.

"Well, first, no matter what account Mr. Morgan has the money hidden in, if it was earned and deposited during the marriage, it's community property. So, at the very least it must be split fifty-fifty. I'm going to subpoena all of his financial records, and I'll need to look at yours as well."

"Okay." One savings account, a car, and a credit card. Not much along the lines of financial records.

"I'm also going to have my investigators find out where he's hiding and who he's hiding with. Proof of any infidelity will help us, too."

I nodded, not sure how to reply.

"Also, I'm going to put you in touch with a good accountant. You need someone to help you with your finances. You've been performing for a long time and although I know you haven't seen Beyoncé-type success, you still should have more to show for it than some clothes, a townhouse, and an Escalade."

"Okay," I replied. Well, she *was* right.

She leaned forward. "Now, the best news of all is that I'm your lawyer, and I *love* taking down men like your husband."

I smiled. "The bad news?"

She reclined in her chair and crossed her legs. "Well, first of all, you trusted your husband. Trust is a good thing in a relationship, but obviously, your husband used your trust against you."

I dropped my eyes.

Shelly continued. "It's going to take a lot of work for us to be ready for the hearing that's coming up, but we *will* be ready.

I raised my eyebrows. "Well, that's a relief."

She smiled and nodded. "But here's the worst news. Your husband greatly underestimates your intelligence, and he thinks that you can't take care of yourself. You see, the worst news is for Mr. Clyde Morgan, because when I'm finished, he'll be in for the shock of his life."

I smiled and nodded again. She was tough alright, scary but tough. "Thank you, Ms. Mixon. I really appreciate you taking my case."

She stood to her feet and returned my smile. "Anything for Reggie. Will you tell him I said hello?"

"Um, actually, he's out there waiting for me now," I said as I pointed towards the outer office.

Her eyes lit up and I sensed that Reggie was more just than a former client to her. "Really?" she asked.

"Yeah."

She followed me out to the waiting area and at seeing each other, both Reggie's and Shelly's faces brightened. Shelly walked over to Reggie, and they embraced each other in a warm hug.

"Oh Reg! Good to see you," Shelly gushed.

"Yeah, you too!" he answered, a little too enthusiastically.

I stood to the side feeling a weird pang of jealousy. It was stupid for me to feel that way. I mean, I was sure that Reggie was past me, and there was no way we could be together anyway. Nevertheless, I was jealous.

I looked over at the receptionist, who gave me an amused look, and then I returned my attention to Reggie and Shelly. They finally released each other, and I guess Reggie remembered that I was standing there.

"Um, so you think you can help Bobbie here?" he asked.

She nodded. "Of course."

"Great."

We all stood there awkwardly silent, and then Reggie said, "Well, I know you're busy. Thanks for helping Bobbie out."

She smiled brightly. "No problem. Call me sometime. We should do lunch."

Reggie smiled warmly. "I'll do it."

Shelly extended her hand to me. "I'll be in touch, Ms. Brooks."

I grasped her hand and answered with, "Okay, thanks."

Reggie walked me out to his vehicle, and once we were inside he asked, "So what do you think of Shelly?"

"Well she she's definitely tough. Tough and frightening."

Reggie laughed. "Yeah, she's not to be messed with. But she's a good lawyer. Believe me, I know."

"Um, Reggie, this is probably none of my business, but is there something going on between you and Ms. Mixon?"

Reggie raised his eyebrows. "Why? You jealous, Superstar?"

I felt my cheeks heat up. "Uh, I was just wondering because she was pretty excited to see you back there."

He shrugged. "Well, I *am* one of her celebrity clients. And I paid her a grip to handle my divorce. She's probably just grateful."

I shook my head. "No, no, Mr. Darrough. That wasn't any lawyer/client appreciation I sensed. That woman has the hots for you."

Reggie laughed. "No, she doesn't."

"Okay, if you say so. Anyway, thanks again, Reggie, for hooking me up with her."

He looked at me, smiled, and said, "Il mio piacere, bella"

I smiled. "What was that?"

"It was Italian for 'my pleasure, beautiful.'"

I blushed. "How do you say 'thank you'?"

"Grazie."

"Grazie," I said.

He grasped my hand and then pulled it up to his lips. "Again, it's my pleasure."

I smiled at him as he released my hand, started the engine, and began driving off the parking lot. At that point, I probably would've done anything Reggie asked me to. Slowly but surely, those old feelings were returning. I turned my head and with a smile on my face, gazed out the window at the Little Rock traffic and before I knew it, the ride had rocked me to sleep. The subject of my dreams? Mr. Reggie Wayne Darrough.

# FOURTEEN

## "Someday After While"

TWO weeks later, I was back in Dr. Barlow's office. I sat directly across from her and filled her in on everything that had been going on in my life: living with Mama, my daily routine, church on Sundays, meeting my divorce lawyer, and the AA meetings. I told her how I'd been able to hire a new manager and a new entertainment lawyer, both of which Reggie found for me. It seemed that he had several friends and connections that I knew nothing about.

"Well, you've certainly been busy," Dr. Barlow said.

I smiled. "Yeah, I have."

"How do you feel about all of these changes happening in your life at the same time?"

"Um, well I guess it actually feels pretty good. You know, like I'm making some progress."

"Progress towards what?"

"Well, a better future; a future where I have more control over what happens in my life."

"I see. Well it certainly sounds like you have a handle on things."

I nodded. "I think I do."

"How are the AA meetings going?"

"To be honest with you, at first I thought that I didn't belong there. But now I can see how it could help me."

Dr. Barlow tilted her head to the left and asked, "Why did you feel like you didn't belong?"

I shrugged. "I know this sounds bad, but I guess I kinda thought that they were way worse off than me. Like I was better than them."

"I see. What changed your mind?"

"I suppose I realized that although I wasn't as deep into addiction as some of those people were, I was on my way there. I had stepped over the edge, and I was on my way down, for sure. Their stories show me where I could end up if I don't get a hold of myself. It made me take a good look at myself."

"What did you see?"

I sighed. "A lot of heartache and pain and other things that I don't like about myself."

"Like what?"

I closed my eyes. "Weakness, mostly. I've been such a weak person for most of my life."

"Weak in what ways?"

I opened my eyes and twisted my mouth. "Well, basically, I gave up control of my life to my husband and before him, my father. In a lot of ways even my career was controlling me. All I did was work. No friends, barely any time off. I was so unhappy."

"Why do you think you gave up that control?"

"I had no self-confidence, and I was afraid of failing, I guess. I was afraid of making a mess of things, so I trusted other people to make all of my decisions for me."

"Do you think you've 'messed things up' in the past, made the wrong decisions?"

I pondered her question for a moment and thought to myself, *what haven't I messed up?*

"Yeah, a lot of things," I said.

"Like what?"

"Um, my relationship with my mom and basically any relationship with any man except my father."

Dr. Barlow leaned forward. "Bobbie, do you think a relationship involves more than one person?"

"Well, yes, of course it does."

"Then how is it that only one person could mess it up?"

I shrugged. "I don't know, but I believe I'm to blame. I'm the common denominator."

Dr. Barlow nodded. "Okay, let's take your relationship with your mom, for instance. How are you solely responsible for your estrangement?"

"Because I'm the opposite of everything she believes in. I've done nothing but disappoint her over and over again. She hates me."

"She's told you this?"

"No, but that's how she treats me. I can feel it. I know she hates me."

"So you assume that she dislikes you based on your perception of how she treats you?"

"Well, yes. How else?"

"Why don't you ask her how she feels about you?"

I vigorously shook my head. "Oh no, I couldn't do that. We don't talk."

"Why not start talking?"

I dropped my eyes and blinked back tears. "I'm afraid to."

"Afraid of rejection? Failure?"

I nodded as the tears began to roll down my cheeks.

Dr. Barlow handed me a tissue and said, "Do you think that it's possible for your relationship with your mom to improve?"

I shook my head as I wiped my face. "No, I don't see how it could."

"Well, it could be as simple as spending a little time with her, getting to know her better, and seeing her real prospective on things. Then maybe you can start a dialogue with her and open the door to healing your relationship."

"Spend time doing what? I mean, I live with the woman right now, *in the same house*. How much more time can I spend with her?" I was beginning to feel a little frustrated.

"Bobbie, do you think that living in the same home automatically means people spend quality time together?"

I thought about me and Clyde. We'd lived in the same home, but I wouldn't call our time together "quality".

"No, not really but what are we supposed to spend time doing? I've spent my whole life singing the blues. That's all I know how to do. My mother is not gonna have anything to do with that. I can tell you that right now."

"Well, maybe you could do something that *she* likes to do. I believe the more time you spend with a person, the more comfortable you become with them which can provide an opening for real conversation."

She might have been right. Although my mom's house was small, we rarely spoke to each other or even sat in the same room together unless it was at the dinner table.

I nodded. "Okay, I see what you're saying. I'll try, but I just don't think it'll work."

"Bobbie, you can only try. No one can fault you for trying."

I nodded. "Yeah."

♫♫♫

Another Saturday morning and my internal alarm clock woke me up at 5:30 A.M. I lay in bed for a moment and then decided to beat Mama to the kitchen. I rose out of bed, wrapped my robe around me, and then stumbled groggily to the kitchen. I fired up the stove and cooked the only thing I ever cooked for breakfast: bacon, scrambled eggs, and toast with butter. By 6:00 A.M., I'd nearly finished cooking and had already set the table. I smiled as Mama walked into the kitchen with a shocked look on her face.

"W...what's going on?" She stuttered.

"Breakfast," I replied with a proud smile.

"You did dis? What's done come over you?" she asked, eyeing the table.

I shrugged, still smiling. "Just thought I'd give you break."

"Well, Lawd know I need one." She stood with her hands clasped in front of her as if she didn't know what to do with herself. "Um, well, lemme go and git the girls."

I shook my head. "You sit down. I'll get 'em."

"Uh, okay."

She took a seat as I walked into the crowded bedroom where Meka and Sharee lay side by side in the queen-sized bed which stood a little shorter than mine. I smiled at the posters that covered the walls; Justin Bieber, the Jonas Brothers, Rihanna. They were fast asleep when I shook them awake. Meka grouchily slid out of bed as Sharee greeted me with a wide smile.

"Good morning," I said cheerfully. "Time for breakfast."

Minutes later, we sat with our heads bowed as Mama said grace. Afterwards, we all dug in and I won rave reviews from the girls. Once breakfast was finished, the girls cleared the table and took care of the dishes.

As Mama stood to leave, I took a deep breath and said, "Um Mama, you wanna go to town today? I'll drive you."

Mama gave me a curious look. "Bobbie Ann, what's goin' on?

*Here we go*, I thought. "Nothing Mama. It's just that if I'm gonna be going to church every Sunday, I need to get some more appropriate clothes."

Mama raised her eyebrows. "Well, I won't argue wit' dat."

*I'm trying, Lord. I really am, but she ain't helping.* "Well, I thought that maybe you and the girls could ride with me."

"I guess I do need ta pick up some thangs. We can leave in a coupla hours if you want."

I smiled. "Okay."

♫♫♫

"Town" was Magnolia, Arkansas. Magnolia was a town of about 12,000 citizens complete with a few department stores and a local college. It was located 20 miles south of Willisville. As a child, Magnolia had seemed like New York City to me. I remembered being so excited about going to town and shopping with my family. You'd have thought I was taking a trip to Disneyworld.

During the drive to the southern Arkansas town, Meka and Sharee kept us entertained with their excited chatter. Their conversation mostly centered on the upcoming fall dance.

"No ma'ams," Mama said. "I ain't lettin' y'all go ta no dance wit' boys. Dat ain't nothin' but trouble."

"Oh please, Grandma?!" Both girls pleaded in unison.

"Naw, I ain't gone be there ta watch y'all," Mama replied while shaking her head.

I glanced at Mama and said. "Well, I could go and watch them. I don't mind. I remember those dances, and I'd hate for them to miss it."

Mama shook her head again. "I jus' don't know."

"I won't let them out of my sight. I promise."

"Pleeeeeease, Granny!" Meka reiterated.

"Well, okay. I guess so," Mama said hesitantly.

The girls squealed with delight, and I smiled.

Once we'd made in to the town square, we immediately hit a couple of stores. I'd received a royalty payment and decided to treat myself. I ended up buying four dresses for myself and two each for Meka and Sharee. Mama refused to let me buy her anything except for lunch at her favorite chicken restaurant.

All in all, it was a good day and Mama was actually pretty cordial with me. She even smiled once or twice. Maybe Dr. Barlow was right. Maybe things really could get better between us. I knew it would definitely take an act of God for us to grow closer, but I have to admit that I had more fun on that day than I'd had in a long time.

# FIFTEEN

## "Still Crazy For You"

ANOTHER week had passed by and the Oak Grove School Fall Dance was gearing up to begin. That evening I stepped out of my bedroom, all dressed up for the dance, and was given an instant stamp of approval from Mama.

"You look real nice, Bobbie Ann," she said, almost sounding like she was surprised.

I was wearing one of the dresses I'd purchased in Magnolia. It was a navy blue polka-dotted, jacket-dress with a red ribbon belt complete with a bow in the back. The A-lined skirt portion fell just below my knees. With it I wore a pair of navy blue pumps. I used a red headband to push back my unruly afro, and I wore simple diamond studs in my ears. I looked like a fifties TV mom, a look that pleased *my* mom.

"Thanks," I replied.

Meka and Sharee emerged from their bedrooms looking sweet in their dresses. Both wore chocolate brown bubble skirts. Meka's blouse was bright yellow and Sharee's mint green. Each wore ribbons in their freshly pressed hair to match their shirts. They were so giddy; I feared they would explode with excitement. We all sat in the den and waited for Reggie, who Mama had asked to drive us to the school in Rosston. After a few moments, a knock was heard at the door. Meka jumped up and opened it without even asking who it was. On the other side of the door stood Reggie, looking like a male model in khaki pants and a yellow polo shirt, a newsboy cap on his head, and a bright smile on his face.

"Y'all ready to get your dance on?" He asked.

"Yeah!" the girls yelled in unison.

"Y'all betta be good, now," Mama warned, with her eyebrows raised.

"They will," I answered.

"Bye, Ms. Mae. I'll have everyone back on time," Reggie said with a smile.

"Okay, see y'all later," Mama replied.

In less than 20 minutes, we'd arrived in Rosston at Oak Grove School. I smiled as we approached the familiar peach-colored frame gym. It seemed much smaller than I'd remembered it, but the campus actually had not changed. A medium-sized beige, cinder block building still housed classrooms for grades Kindergarten through six and across the road, an identical building housed grades seven through twelve. The old gym stood on the elementary side. Reggie pulled to a stop on the gravel parking lot and then hopped out and opened the doors for me and the girls. Kids in grades six through twelve were invited to the dance, and it looked like most all of them had shown up.

Reggie laughed as Meka and Sharee hurriedly walked into the gym ahead of us, their shiny patent leather shoes reflecting the lights that hung on either side of the gym doors. We walked inside to find the gym festively decorated with brown crepe streamers and orange and yellow balloons. Several teachers and parents were seated on the old wooden bleachers as the kids crowded the dance floor. The DJ, one of the coaches, was blasting a Beyoncé song. Reggie smiled at me and gestured towards the bleachers on the right side of the gym. I nodded and we walked over and took a seat near the middle of the basketball court.

I watched the girls like a hawk, but they were good girls, and not one time did I see them misbehave. We had arrived at 7:00 P.M. and by 8:00 P.M., the dance was in full swing. The children danced and laughed and talked and basically just had a really good time. I caught myself smiling more than once. I guess their happiness was just infectious. I sat there with Reggie by my side and thoroughly enjoyed myself.

Around 8:30, the night began to wind down and the DJ announced that he was taking his final requests. Reggie jumped up and whispered in my ear that he would be right back. I figured that he was going to the restroom or something and continued to watch the kids. Moments later, he returned with a grin on his face. I gave him a curious look, and then I heard the song begin to play.

"Slow Jam? Like senior prom?" I asked.

His grin widened as he nodded. "Yeah, the Monica and Usher version. The one you like." He extended his hand. "May I have this dance, Ms. Brooks?"

I sat there and wondered how he could have remembered that song. I had nearly forgotten about it myself, and there wasn't much about my relationship with Reggie that I didn't remember.

"Um, I'm supposed to be watching the girls, not dancing," I said, feeling a little nervous about being so close to Reggie.

"We can watch them even better from the dance floor."

I glanced at the kids on the floor. "Uh, I don't know."

He leaned in close to my ear and said, "One dance?"

I hesitated as the sensation of his warm breath on my ear startled me, and then I agreed. "Ok, one dance."

He closed his eyes and nodded his head. "Thank you, Ms. Brooks."

I took his hand and we stepped onto the worn, but shiny oak gym floor. I placed my hands on Reggie's shoulders, which was a stretch for me. After all, he was more than a foot taller than me. As the music played, we swayed back and forth, and I have to admit that it felt pretty good to feel his hands on my hips. At first, I kept my eyes on the girls, but by the middle of the song, I was lost in the music and had closed my eyes.

We continued to dance. I felt Reggie pull me closer and closer until finally, I felt his body press against mine. I laid my head on his chest, and he wrapped his arms around me. It was the safest feeling I'd felt in a long time. It felt so good that I wished the song would never end, but of course it did. The music faded out and Reggie released me. I looked up at him and he gazed into my eyes with the sweetest expression on his face.

"That was nice," he said, barely above a whisper.

"Uh, yeah, it was. It…it was real nice." I replied softly.

After the dance, Reggie drove us straight home as promised. An exhausted Meka and Sharee walked into the house and went straight to bed. Reggie walked me to the door and then took my hand and kissed it.

"Thanks for the ride, Reg," I said.

"Thanks for the dance," he said through a slight grin.

"Yeah, well I enjoyed it myself."

He raised his eyebrows. "Really? Well, we'll have to do it again sometimes."

I nodded. "Okay."

I reached up and hugged Reggie's neck and then stepped back and said, "Goodnight, Reggie."

"Goodnight, Bobbie Ann. I'mma hold you to that dance."

I smiled. "Okay."

♫♫♫

Sunday consisted of church, of course, and then a dinner of fried pork chops, pinto beans, collard greens, and cornbread. My contribution was the cornbread, but I assisted with everything else. I was actually beginning to enjoy being in the kitchen with Mama. Believe it or not, we had actually begun talking to each other. I mean, we weren't having marathon conversations or sharing deep secrets, but we would talk about the sermon or whatever was on TV and sometimes she even shared the local gossip with me; he was creeping with her or she left him for him. For such a small place, enough drama went on in Willisville to fill a full season of soap operas.

After dinner, I sat on the sofa and watched an old black and white movie with Mama who was busy shelling some peas. It was a romance, and Mama seemed to thoroughly enjoy it. I wondered if Mama ever dated after Daddy. In the month I'd been back home, she hadn't had even one phone call from a man, let alone a visit. I didn't dare ask her. Things were going better between us, and I didn't want to risk getting on her bad side by delving into her personal business.

Once the movie had ended, I hopped up off of the couch and went to my room with full intentions of taking a nap. It was just four in the afternoon, but all that food had made me sleepy. I went into the room and glanced at my cell phone on the dresser. I was shocked to see that there was one missed call. I picked the phone up and was even more shocked when I saw that the call had been from Clyde. I nearly dropped the phone and had to lean against the bed and catch my breath as I felt my heart race. I read the number over and over again to be sure. It was definitely Clyde, but why was he calling, and why now? I wasn't exactly sure what to do. Should I call him back?

I stared at the phone for a few minutes and then decided to see if he'd left a message. Sure enough, he had. I held the phone to my ear and listened as he spoke.

"Baby girl, it's me, Clyde. Um, we need to talk. Call me back as soon as possible. I really need to talk to you," he said. He sounded like nothing had happened between us. Like he hadn't deserted me and cleaned out all of our accounts.

I stood there and clutched the phone and the more I thought about the call and the message, the angrier I became. The nerve of him! Did he think that he could just call and I'd be willing to talk to him? And exactly what did we have to talk about, anyway?

I grabbed my denim jacket and shoved my feet into a pair of sneakers. I headed out the side door and into the afternoon air after telling Mama I was going for a walk. She gave me a curious look and nodded in response.

Once outside, I put my cell phone in my pocket and began to walk down the driveway in the direction of nowhere in particular. I looked down at the ground and kicked at the rocks as I fought the temptation to either find a drink or call and cuss Clyde out. I knew that neither would be a good thing to do.

I continued to walk down the driveway and once I'd reached the end, I turned left and headed down the short road that led to the main road. After a few more minutes of walking, I stepped onto the main road and continued my trek.

I had been on the main road for a few minutes when I heard rapidly falling footsteps behind me growing closer and closer. I stopped in my tracks and turned around with a frown on my face. My expression softened as I saw Reggie trotting towards me wearing a white t-shirt and the black slacks he'd worn to church.

"You out jogging in your good church shoes?" I asked, pointing at the shiny black boats that were covering his huge feet.

He smiled and breathing heavily, said, "Naw, I was just trying to catch up with you."

I grinned back. That smile of his was something else. "Oh. How'd you know I was out here?"

"I was up at the church. I saw you when you passed by."

"Oh, I didn't see your truck."

He nodded. "It's parked behind the church. Uh, where you headed?"

I shrugged and softly said, "I honestly don't know."

He grabbed my hand. "Then come with me."

I raised my eyebrows. "Where?"

He grinned. "Just come on, you'll see."

I stood there and looked at him for a moment.

"Come on, Superstar."

I smiled a little and with some hesitation, I followed Reggie as he turned in the direction of my mother's property. Soon we began to approach the church and my curiosity got the best of me.

"Are we going to the church?" I asked.

Reggie laughed and shook his head. "No, no, don't worry. We're not going *near* the church."

I swatted his arm. "I didn't mean it like that, Reggie." But I guess I *had* made it seem like the worst place in the world to me.

He chuckled and said, "I know. Come on."

We continued on behind the church and then onto a narrow path that led into the wooded area which served as a backdrop to the church.

I smiled. "Oh, I know where we're going," I said barely above a whisper.

Reggie smiled down at me and squeezed my hand as he continued to guide me along the path which seemed much smaller than I remembered it. Either that or maybe I was just bigger. But I imagined that no one had been down that path in a long while. I doubted members of the younger generation even knew that it existed.

It seemed as if we were on an endless path as we trudged up and down small hills and around curves and bends, with Reggie pushing low hanging branches from oak and pine trees out of our way. I held tightly onto his hand as we walked. I felt completely safe with him.

A smile spread across my face as Reggie stopped at the top of a steep hill and pointed.

"Our spot," he said softly and then smiled down at me.

Below us was a small, lush green clearing and at the center of it was a natural spring. At the center of the spring, the water bubbled to the surface creating small ripples in the water. Reggie slowly led me down the hill and over to a huge old uprooted pine tree. When we were younger, the tree proved to be an adequate bench for us. On this day, that tree would serve the exact same purpose.

Reggie sat down and tugged on my hand, signaling me to take a seat next to him. The woods were silent except for the occasional bird call or the sound of a small animal scurrying up or down a tree. And of course, the soothing sounds of the spring filled the air. We sat quietly for a long while, holding hands and staring at the spring. It was both beautiful and peaceful.

Breaking the silence, I began to softly hum a tune. It was an old song that had been one of my father's favorites of mine.

"What's that?" Reggie asked softly.

"What's what?" I asked.

He offered me a sweet smile. "That song you were humming."

I shrugged. "Oh just a song I wrote a long time ago. It's kinda sad, really."

"You recorded it?"

I shook my head. "Naw, it got cut from my first album before it was released. The record company said it wasn't 'bluesy enough'. It's still one of my favorites, though. It was one of my daddy's favorites, too."

"Well, what's the name of it?"

I stared at the water in from of us and said, "I Wish."

"Sing it for me."

"Really? I don't know. I haven't really sung anything in a while now. Not since I've been home."

He nodded enthusiastically. "Yeah really, I want you to sing it for me. Bless me with that voice of yours, Superstar."

I smiled then took a deep breath and began to sing for the first time in weeks. I closed my eyes and let the words slide off of my tongue and to be truthful, although the lyrics were sad, it made me feel pretty good. Singing was my thing, and it always had the power to lift my mood.

*"I'm here all alone*
*Just as you left me*
*Gone is our song*
*I miss the way that you loved me*

*I wish you were here*
*Need you now, to hold me*
*I miss you, my dear*
*No one else even really knows me*

*I'm so lost, so lost without you*
*My heart cries and aches so bad*
*No more smiles or laughter are in me*
*Because I miss you, baby I'm so sad*

*I wish for you back*
*I wish for us, I do*
*I wish you'd love me*

*Again like you used to…"*

When I'd finished singing, I opened my eyes and looked at Reggie. He was staring at me like I was the only thing in his world at that moment.

He grasped both of my hands and said, "That was beautiful, Bobbie Ann. Not like any blues song I've ever heard."

"Um, well thanks, Reggie. It probably would've been better with music though. You know, a guitar or a keyboard."

He shook his head. "I don't see how it could've been any more beautiful than it was."

I smiled shyly. "Well, thanks."

"When did you say you wrote that?"

I dropped my eyes. "A long time ago. Some years back."

"How many years back?"

"Like around twelve years ago."

Reggie dropped his gaze as well. "Like when I left?"

I nodded. "Yeah."

Reggie leaned forward and looked right into my eyes. "Bobbie, I wanna apologize to you."

I furrowed my brow. "For what?"

"For the way things ended between us. I'm so sorry."

I smiled. "Oh Reggie, we were just kids. Yeah, I was sad when I wrote that song, but it's okay now. Really it is."

He shook his head. "No, Bobbie, just let me do this," he said with urgency in his voice and his eyes.

"Okay," I said with a sigh.

"I loved you, I really did and I still do." He let go of my hands and leaned forward with his elbows on his knees and his head in his hands. "I just got up at that college, and it was so different, you know? Those girls were all over me, and I just lost myself. I didn't write or call, and I'm sorry."

I placed my hand on his back. "I understand. You were just a kid."

"I don't want to make any excuses for myself. I should've made time to write you back or visit. By the time I got to missing you and decided to call, your mom said you were out on the road."

I frowned and said, "You called me? Mama never told me."

He ran his fingers through his hair and looked up at me. "Yeah, I tried. I shoulda done more than that, though. I shoulda married you. If I had, neither of us would be where we are now."

I shook my head. "Reggie, it's alright, really. I'm where I'm at because of the decisions I made for myself. That's not your fault." *Tell him*, a voice inside of me said.

He placed his hand on my shoulder. "I'm so sorry. I see you in all this pain. The way he treated you? I feel like it's my fault. I shoulda been there for you. You shoulda been *my* wife," His voice broke as he spoke.

I stared at him for a moment. *Tell him.* "Look Reggie, I loved you too, but we were just too young. It just wasn't meant to be."

Reggie sat up straight and turned towards me. "Bobbie Ann?"

I searched his eyes and said, "Yeah?"

He stared at me for a moment, and I dropped my eyes. I took a deep breath and released it. I knew I had to tell him, especially since he was so full of guilt.

He had still not spoken when I said, "Um Reggie, I need to tell you—"

At that moment, he pulled me into a kiss and abruptly interrupted my confession. My first reaction was shock. I stared at him wide-eyed and wondered what was going on. But as he pulled me closer to him, I closed my eyes and felt my body relax against his. He caressed my back as he held me and to say that he felt good was an understatement. When he finally released me, I sprung to my feet, and stumbled backwards, shaking my head.

"W…what was that? What are you doing?" *Are preachers supposed to kiss like that?* I wondered.

Reggie looked at me with love pouring from his eyes. "Didn't you hear me? I love you, Bobbie Ann. I never stopped loving you." His voice was barely above a whisper.

I squeezed my eyes shut. "But you can't, you shouldn't. Why would you? I'm not what you think I am. I'm not the same Bobbie Ann from twelve years ago. I've done bad things, horrible things. You deserve better, Reggie. You really do. You're too good for me."

His eyes searched mine as he stood up and placed his hands on my shoulders. "I don't care about the things you've done. I love you, and you love me, too. I can feel it."

I shook my head. "Reggie, I don't really know how I feel about anything, right now. Everything's just so confusing. I'm a mess right now."

"Okay," he said quietly, then looked away and sat back down on the log.

Lord knows that I didn't want to hurt him, but we couldn't be together. We just couldn't. I reclaimed my seat next to him on the log, and we sat quietly for the next few moments. I couldn't look at him. I knew I'd hurt his feelings.

"Reggie," I said, staring down at my hands in my lap. "I know it took a lot for you to say what you did, and I'm sorry if I hurt your feelings. I didn't mean—"

Reggie stood up and interrupted me. "It's alright. Lemme get you home. Ms. Mae'll be worried."

I stood up and looked at him. He looked away. "Reggie, I'm really sorry," I said as I reached up and touched his cheek. "Look, deep inside, I've always loved you, Reggie, and I always will. But that doesn't change the fact that I'm no good for you." I shook my head. "No good at all."

He cupped my face in his hands. "Why don't you let me be the judge of that? I'm a big boy, you know." He leaned in and planted a soft kiss on my lips. "We belong together, Bobbie. I know it. I feel it in my soul."

I sighed. "Reggie, I—"

He placed a finger on my lips to silence me. "No more. Let's go, Superstar."

It was getting dark outside. He led me back down the path and all the way to my mother's house. Outside the door, he kissed me again.

"Goodnight, Bobbie Ann," he whispered.

"Goodnight, Reggie," I said.

I walked into the house and went straight to my bedroom with a faint smile on my face. As I settled into bed, not one thought of Clyde or his phone call entered my mind. It seemed that Reggie had swept my blues away.

# SIXTEEN

### "That's Alright"

I twisted around in my seat and craned my neck until I could see Reggie sitting at the very back of the courtroom. Reggie, who already had his eyes fixed on me, smiled and nodded at me. I offered him a weak smile and then turned and looked at Clyde who sat across the aisle from me dressed like a respectable businessman. His lawyer was at his side. Directly behind him sat Sabrina, my former back-up singer. Well, that explained a lot. No wonder she always had an attitude with me and no wonder she and Clyde disappeared at the same time back in Chicago. Well, I could tell her, Clyde wasn't much to steal from a person. Not much at all.

Shelly tapped me on my shoulder and jerked me out of my thoughts.

I gave her a wide-eyed expression as she spoke. "Good news," she whispered. "We've got Judge Elliott. She'll be very sympathetic to you."

I nodded. I sure hoped that Shelly knew what she was talking about, but I had a feeling that she did. Sitting next to me in a brown pin-striped pant-suit and burnt orange blouse, Shelly Mixon exuded pure confidence, a characteristic that I wished I possessed more of.

As Judge Elliott walked into the Dallas courtroom, everyone stood to receive her. Judge Myra Elliott was a middle-aged African American woman who wore her thick, red hair in a low-cut afro. She was attractive, but stern looking, sort of how you'd expect a judge to look. She took her seat behind the bench, peered over her round, gold-trimmed eyeglasses, and instructed the court to be seated.

"Your Honor, first case on the docket is Morgan vs. Brooks," the bailiff announced.

"Are all parties present?" the judge inquired.

"Yes, Your Honor and they've been sworn in," the bailiff answered.

"Very well. I see that Mr. Clyde Morgan is petitioning the court for the dissolution of his marriage to Bobbie Brooks. Does Ms. Brooks have any objections to this petition or request an attempt at reconciliation?"

Shelly stood and addressed the court. "Your Honor, Shelly Mixon, counsel for Ms. Brooks."

The judge nodded. "Ms. Mixon."

"Your Honor, Ms. Brooks does not believe that the marriage can be saved and would like to countersue for divorce on the grounds of abandonment," Shelly said.

"I see. Then we will proceed." Judge Elliott turned to Clyde's table. "Mr. Martin, you may begin."

Clyde's lawyer stood from the table and began to speak. "Yes, Your Honor, Andrew Martin, counsel for Mr. Morgan. Um, you will see in the petition that Mr. Morgan and Ms. Brooks have no children from this marriage. As far as property goes, Mr. Morgan wishes to retain his vehicle and the property he and Ms. Brooks shared here in Dallas. He is also seeking spousal maintenance from Ms. Brooks as he devoted himself to her and her career during the marriage and was not otherwise employed during the marriage."

"I see," said Judge Elliott "Ms. Mixon?"

Shelly stood and balanced her weight on the heel of one of her copper pumps. She glanced at Clyde's attorney and then began speaking. "Your Honor, Ms. Brooks is not an unreasonable woman. She wishes that all of the couple's property be sold and the proceeds be split evenly. She wishes to retain her vehicle and she does not object to Mr. Morgan retaining his. We do, however, object to Mr. Morgan's petition for spousal maintenance. Mr. Morgan has served as Ms. Brooks' manager for twelve years and it was only after he abandoned her, cleaned out all of their joint accounts, effectively leaving her penniless, and filed for divorce that she fired him. Mr. Morgan is a music industry veteran and we are sure that he will not find it difficult to secure future employment.

"Furthermore, we ask that the court review Mr. Morgan's financial records so that Ms. Brooks is ensured to receive what she has worked so hard for. We ask that Mr. Morgan be ordered to turn over all monies earned by Bobbie Brooks except for the 30% to which Mr. Morgan is entitled as having served as her manager. As I mentioned before, Ms. Brooks is under new management and Mr. Morgan is not entitled to any of her future earnings."

Judge Elliott nodded. "I see that there is a lot to consider here. I will give you all three weeks to gather all of the information needed to support your claims. Mr. Morgan and Ms. Brooks, you are both ordered to turn over complete financial records for my consideration by that date as well as records of any property obtained during the marriage. We will reconvene in four weeks and at that time, I will render my decision," with a bang of her gavel, she added, "You are dismissed."

I stood, breathed a sigh of relief, and shook Shelly's hand. "Thank you so much. At least this part is over."

She smiled. "Oh honey, I eat men like Mr. Martin and Mr. Morgan for breakfast. Don't you worry about a thing. We'll come out on top. There's no doubt about that."

I smiled and nodded, afraid to say anything else. Shelly Mixon was one bad chick, alright. I turned and for a second locked eyes with Clyde. He quickly looked away. I turned to see Reggie walking towards me.

"Hey," he said as he took my hand. "You okay?"

I nodded. "I'm better than I thought I'd be."

"Good," he said and then looked at Shelly. "Hey, Shelly. Thanks a lot."

She flashed him a warm smile. "Anything for a friend of yours. And thanks for lunch the other day."

I raised my eyebrows and looked at Reggie. Lunch, huh?

"No problem. I enjoyed it," Reggie replied with a smile.

Shelly turned to me. "I'll be in touch, Ms. Brooks."

I nodded. "Okay, thanks again."

"No problem," Shelly said and then began gathering her paperwork and briefcase.

Reggie walked me out of the courthouse and once we were inside his vehicle, he asked, "You hungry?"

"What, no lunch with Ms. Mixon today?" I asked with my eyebrows raised.

He smiled widely. "Jealous again? I'm flattered, but you gotta know that I'm not into the fembot-lawyer types. Give me a soft, curvy, blues singer any day."

I smiled and looked down at my hands in my lap. "I could eat, I guess. I know a really good barbecue place not far from here. They got good ribs there."

"Okay," he said, then suddenly appearing to be nervous, he added, "Um I need to ask you something first."

"Oh, okay," I said.

Reggie lifted his long body off of his seat and reached into the hip pocket of his black slacks, unearthing a small black box. A *ring* box. I bucked my eyes. Was he really going to do what it looked like he was going to do?

"Bobbie Brooks, will you marry me?" Yeah, he did it. I looked down at the box as he opened it to reveal an absolutely lovely ring.

I held my hand up to my mouth and replied with a muffled, "Reggie, are you serious?"

He nodded, never taking his eyes off of my face. "Well yeah. I don't usually play about these things, you know."

"Why?"

"Why what? You mean, why do I wanna marry you?"

I nodded. "Yeah, I mean, I don't understand why you would want someone like me."

"Because you're special. You're beautiful and talented and you have a good heart. Besides all that, I love you and I can't see myself with anyone else. God made us for each other, Bobbie Ann. I know that as well as I know my name."

I moved my hand from my mouth to my forehead. "Um, Reggie, I'm still married to Clyde Morgan. I can't get *engaged*. That would be totally out of order. Besides, you're a preacher and I'm a blues singer. It'll never work."

Reggie frowned. "Says who?"

"The world and society as a whole. I'm a wretch, Reggie. I really am. You deserve better. I'm damaged goods."

"First of all, I don't give a damn about what the world or society has to say about anything. I'm not *of* the world, my dear."

I raised my eyebrows. "Can preachers say 'damn'?" I asked.

"I just did, didn't I? I'm not just a preacher; I'm a man. I love you and you love me. That's why it *will* work."

I sighed. "Reggie, I just don't know."

He laid the ring box down on the dashboard and grabbed my hand. "Look, Bobbie. I want to marry you and be there for you and take care of you. I want to have a bunch of babies and grow old with you."

I swallowed hard and shook my head. "That all sounds nice and I have no doubt that you mean it, but I can't just rush from one marriage into another one. I need to know that I can take care of myself and stand on my own two feet. I've depended on others way too much in my life."

He nodded. "I understand that and I'm not trying to pressure you. Can I tell you something, Bobbie?"

I nodded in response, still shocked at his proposition.

He leaned close to me and lowered his voice. "When I was a little kid, my grandma used to go fishing all the time. Most of the time, she took me with her. Sometimes she'd have some good luck and catch dinner for us; others, we'd sit out on the banks of some creek or lake for hours without a single bite. You know what that taught me? It taught me great patience. I'm a patient man and the thought of waiting doesn't bother me. Because I understand how valuable you are, how much you mean to me." He leaned closer to me until his lips gently brushed mine.

I closed my eyes and when I opened them, I watched as he picked up the ring box, closed it, and then opened the glove box.

He smiled at me and said, "I'm gonna lock it in this glove box. When you're ready, it'll be here." He set the ring box inside and then locked the glove compartment. "I can wait. I've got nothing but time."

I nodded and stared out the window as we headed to Curry's Rib Shack. My mind was reeling from the events of the day, not the least of which was Reggie's proposal. I closed my eyes and tried to figure out what to do with my life. I did care about Reggie; that much was undeniable. But I was just afraid, so very afraid to be with him.

# SEVENTEEN

## "Please Accept My Love"

I sat up in bed, reading over some of the 12-step literature, hoping that I'd eventually read myself to sleep. We were up to step eight and I felt like I was making good progress. I was even getting to know some of the other participants and thought that maybe some real friendships could come out of this experience. Over the past years, I'd worked at a constant pace, making it difficult to make friends. Really, the only friendships I'd managed to create were the ones with my band members. A couple of them had called and checked on me since I'd been in Arkansas.

Therapy was going well, too. It actually felt pretty good having someone to open up to, and work through my issues with. I was discovering a lot of interesting things about myself, some of which I didn't want to know, but definitely needed to know.

I set down the pamphlet I was reading and picked up my notebook, which was filled with some songs and poems. Some were completed and others weren't. I flipped through the pages until I found a blank page and then I picked up my pen.

Step eight was "Made a list of all persons we had harmed and became willing to make amends to them all." I took a deep breath and then began to make my list. Number one was Reggie. If I'd ever wronged anyone, I'd definitely wronged him. Next was Clyde. Yes, he'd been a terrible husband to me, but I had to admit, I wouldn't have won any awards in the "good wife" category either. The list continued with Mama and then Daddy. I really wondered if I had made Daddy proud to be my father. Had I really made the right choices in my life?

Even though Mama had never been very warm towards me over the years, I'd never made any big effort to open up to her either. Basically, I had ignored her and left her out of most of my life. Next on the list was God. Well, He really should've been first on the list. But, anyway, in the past, I hadn't even tried to consider Him in my decisions. What little I'd learned about God as a child had been totally ignored. The more I listened to the sermons at church and the more I was around Reggie's kind and peaceful nature, the more I realized that God is really the center of everything and that without Him, nothing is worthwhile.

The last name on the list was mine. The way I'd lived my life up to that point had robbed me of happiness and peace. I'd spent the better of my time pursuing success in my career, but what had I lost in the process? Even my marriage had been arranged to further my career. I tapped my lips with the pen as I thought about what I'd written. I was startled out of deep thought by a tapping at my window.

I frowned and crawled to the foot of the bed. I pushed the red and white lace curtains to the side and peeped out the window. It was Reggie, dressed in all black and grinning from ear to ear. I smiled and shook my head as I quickly slid out of bed. It was 10:00 P.M., according to my cell phone, and Mama and the girls were already fast asleep.

I pulled a sweater on over my pajamas and slipped on a pair of mule-style sneakers then quietly crept through then den and out to the carport to meet Reggie. As soon as I shut the door behind me, Reggie stepped from the front of the house and walked under the carport with his hands hidden behind his back. He leaned over and kissed me on the cheek.

"Reggie Darrough, what are you doing?" I asked.

"I just wanted to see my girl," he said.

"Okay, but don't you see me like every day?"

"Well, actually, I was talking about Ms. Mae."

I rolled my eyes. "Oh, really?"

He laughed softly. "Well, Ms. Mae *is* special to me, but you know I only have eyes for some Bobbie Ann."

I smiled up at him. "You're not tired of seeing this old face by now?"

He leaned over and kissed me softly on the lips this time. "I dream about that face all the time. I missed you tonight. You missed me, too."

I raised my eyebrows. "Wow, I like the way you think you can tell me how I'm feeling."

He grinned. "Well you did, didn't you?"

I looked down at my feet, suddenly feeling shy. "Yeah, I guess I did."

"I knew it." He bent over and kissed me again.

"Reggie, what are you hiding behind your back?" I asked once our lips had parted.

"Oh yeah." He pulled his hand from behind his back to reveal a single pink rose. "For you. A flower for a flower."

"Um, Reg? Did you pick that off of one of my mama's bushes?"

He grinned sheepishly. "Yeah."

"Wow, you're cheap, Mr. Baller, shot caller," I joked.

"Well, I was actually going for romantic and spontaneous, not cheap. But if you want, I'll buy a truckload of roses and have 'em delivered to you one by one."

I smiled. "You are crazy, Reggie Darrough." I took the rose from him. "Why are you really here, though?"

He looked at me and placed his hands on my arms. "I was at Mama's watching TV and your face popped into my head. Well truthfully, I think about you all the time." He moved his hands to my cheeks. "I wanted to come over here and tell you that I love you."

I looked him in the eye. "Really?"

"Mm hmm. I wanted to look into your eyes when I said it. And I also wanted to do this."

As he held my face in his huge hands, he brought his face close to me and allowed his lips to barely brush mine. I placed my hands over his as he leaned in and kissed me with such passion that my knees buckled and my legs nearly gave way. He continued to kiss me, his hands moving from my face to my hips. He gripped me tightly and kissed me until he was satisfied and then he released me.

"Uh, I…" was all I could manage to utter.

He smiled. "Let me know when you're ready for me, Superstar."

He turned to leave and I grabbed his hand. He turned back around and gave me a curious look. I reached up and kissed him. He pulled me close to him and held me as we kissed for what felt like hours. In all the years we were married, Clyde had never, ever made me feel like that. At that moment, I probably would've done anything Reggie asked me to do, good or bad.

Our kiss finally ended and I whispered, "Goodnight, Reggie."

He tapped the tip of my nose with his fingertip. "Goodnight, Bobbie Ann."

I watched as he walked across the yard to the church, where he'd parked his truck. Then I slipped back into the house and into bed. As I laid my head on the pillow I smiled and thanked God for Reggie Darrough and I wondered why he loved me so much when I didn't deserve it.

♫♫♫

The next morning, after we'd finished breakfast, I stood up from the table and quietly began gathering up the dishes. When the girls left to get ready for school, Mama walked into the kitchen behind me with a handful of dishes.

She handed them to me and said, "Tell Reggie Darrough not to be sneakin' around my property stealin' roses off my bushes."

I nearly dropped the glass I was washing. I turned and looked at Mama and she was actually smiling at me.

"I…I thought you were sleep. You knew he was here?" I asked.

"Humph. I heard 'em when he pulled up to da church. I'mma old goat. Ain't no foolin' me."

I smiled. "Mama, what do you think about Reggie?" I already knew the answer to that question.

"Reggie a good man and he deserve a good woman," she answered.

"Yeah, I know."

"Why you ask den?"

"Um, he says he loves me and he asked me to marry him."

Mama nearly dropped the jar of jelly she held in *her* hand. "What chu say when he ask you dat?"

I shrugged. "I told him I'm not ready."

"Well, how you feel 'bout him, Bobbie Ann? You love 'em?"

"I don't think I ever stopped loving Reggie. Not even when me and Clyde were together. I just don't wanna hurt him."

Mama placed the jelly in the door of the refrigerator and then shut it. She turned to me with a concerned look on her face. "Why you think you gone hurt 'em? You thinkin' 'bout takin' Clyde back."

I couldn't tell her the truth, so I just shook my head and said, "Lord no. Me and Clyde are over. I guess I'm just scared."

"Well, take yo' time and make yo' mind up. Either you wit' 'em or you ain't. Don't play wit 'em and don't use 'em to git over yo' husband. He don't deserve dat."

"Yes ma'am." I turned the water on to rinse the dishes and then turned to Mama and asked, "Mama, you ever think about dating or getting married again?"

She shook her head. "I used ta, right after yo' daddy passed. I was real lonely den. But now, I think it's best I stay da way I am."

"Don't you ever get lonely now?"

Mama sighed. "Well, yeah but I got da girls and my job and church. If da Lawd got somebody for me, he gone send 'em. No need in worrin' on it. Yo' daddy was a good man. Be hard ta find another one like 'em."

I glanced towards the girls' room and lowered my voice. "Do Earl Jr. and Nora Lee ever check on the girls?"

She shook her head. "Ain't checked on dem in years. It's probly for da best though. When they did come 'round they was only looking for money." She paused and shook her head. "I don't even know if dat boy is living or dead now."

"What happened to him? How'd he end up like this? He was always so smart, brilliant really."

"Same thang dat happened to you. The pressures of life got to 'em. He got up there at State College and let da' pressure get to 'em.

All I know ta do is pray for 'em and hope dat one day he'll find hisself again and find Jesus."

"Yeah, I guess that's all any of us can do, pray."

"Prayin' is always da' best thang ta do."

"Mama, how'd you get so strong?"

"Nothin' but Jesus, baby. Nothin' but Jesus."

# EIGHTEEN

## "You've Got To Hurt Before You Heal"

I walked into Dr. Barlow's inviting office and took my usual seat across from her. She smiled that warm smile of hers and greeted me.

"Bobbie, how are you today?"

I gave her a smile of my own. "I'm okay."

"Good. How have things been going?"

I shrugged. "Um, I'm not sure what the word is. Strange, I guess."

She raised her eyebrows and nodded. "Strange is an interesting choice of words. Why strange?"

I filled her in on the progression of my relationship with my mother, the divorce hearing, and Reggie's proposal.

"Well, things certainly have been interesting for you, haven't they?" she asked.

I nodded in agreement. "Very interesting."

"Well, let's start with the hearing. How did it feel seeing your husband after all this time?"

"Um, weird, but not as painful as I'd thought it'd be."

"Why do you think that is?"

I shrugged. "I don't know. Maybe I never really loved him?"

"Do you believe that?"

I sat and pondered that question for a moment and then said, "Yeah, I think I do believe it. I needed someone to take care of me at the time, and Clyde fit the bill. My mama told me that needing someone isn't the same as loving someone."

"I see. So you're saying that you never loved him at all?"

I shook my head. "I'm not saying that. I did love him in a way, but it was only for what he could do for me, not for who he was as a person."

"So you used him?"

I was taken aback by that statement. "Wow, I guess you could say that. It sounds kinda harsh when you put it that way, but I suppose it's the truth. We basically used each other. Talk about a dysfunctional relationship." I shook my head in disgust.

"What about Reggie?" she queried.

"What about him?" I asked.

"How do you feel about him?"

I smiled. "He's great, a good man. He's kind, considerate, and patient and I really believe that he loves me."

"And you? Do you love him?"

"I *wanna* love him. I was very much in love with him when we were younger, and I know he's in my heart. But…"

"But what?"

I dropped my eyes to the floor. "But there's something in our past that I haven't told him. Something that I don't wanna tell him."

"Why?"

"I'm afraid to."

She leaned forward. "Bobbie, what could be so bad that you can't share it with a man whom you know loves you?"

I sighed. "It'll hurt him. It's nearly killed me to carry it around all these years. I just don't want him to have to deal with it." I wiped a single tear from my cheek.

Dr. Barlow gave me a concerned look. "Have you told *anyone*?"

I shook my head. "No." My voice broke as I answered her.

"Bobbie, do you feel safe here in my office?"

I nodded. "Yes."

"And you know that whatever you tell me stays here? Everything is strictly confidential."

I nodded again.

"Do you want to tell me?" she asked while handing me a tissue.

"I don't know. I've kept it a secret for so long. Maybe saying it out loud will make it seem too real to me."

"And by keeping it a secret, has that made it any less real?"

I shook my head as I wiped my eyes. "No, it hasn't."

I took a deep breath and closed my eyes and began to speak. It felt like her office had transformed into a confessional for a moment in time as I poured my heart out and tearfully emptied my soul of the burden I'd carried alone for more that twelve years. When I was finished, Dr. Barlow gave me a moment to pull myself together, offered me some words of encouragement, and then escorted me out of the safety of her office and back into the reality of the world.

The ride home was a quiet and serene one. Having seen my tear-streaked face and puffy eyes as I emerged from Dr. Barlow's office, Reggie had simply taken my hand in his and led me to his vehicle. Without a word, he'd driven me home and once we'd arrived at Mama's, he'd planted a soft kiss on my lips and then left me with a promise to check on me later.

He was good to me and he loved me, this much I knew to be true. As I headed into the house and lay across my bed, I offered a prayer to God. I asked him to forgive me for what I'd done and to give me the strength and courage to tell Reggie. I knew I had to tell him the truth, because I knew how very much he cared for me. I cared for him, too, but I was still unsure if I could love him the way he deserved to be loved.

# NINETEEN

### "Cheaper to Keep Her"

REGGIE and I walked into the Dallas courtroom hand in hand. Once inside, Reggie bent over, smiled at me, and kissed me on the cheek before I left him to take my seat next to Shelly. She had been keeping me informed of the progress of my case. I was surprised to find out that Clyde had amassed quite an empire during our marriage. In addition to the townhouse we'd shared, Clyde owned other property including a house in Houston and a plot of land in Tennessee. He was also part owner in a couple of franchise businesses.

It also seemed that he'd been skimming off of the money in our accounts and squirreling it away for years. The sum total of all of Clyde's personal accounts totaled more than three million dollars. That was far more than the 30% he should have earned as my manager. 30% was a ridiculous cut for a manager, and I knew it, but he was my husband and my partner of sorts. But on my best day, I hadn't earned enough for his cut to be that large. In addition to all of that, Shelly's investigator had also uncovered that Clyde and Sabrina had been having an affair for more than a year. He had also been financially supporting her, it seems, with *my* money.

As I settled into my seat, I glanced across at Clyde who in turn flashed me a smile. I frowned and wondered what he was up to. I looked at the seats behind him. No Sabrina. As a matter of fact, I didn't see her anywhere in the room. Was there trouble in paradise so soon?

I looked back at Reggie, who, dressed in a gray suit and pink dress shirt, looked like a handsome business man. He flashed me a brilliant smile which I returned, and then I turned around in my seat just in time for the bailiff to announce the entrance of Judge Elliott. I stood from my seat next to Shelly and nervously tapped my high-heeled foot. I really could not wait for all of it to be over. Shelly looked sharp as she stood next to me in a white linen pant-suit.

I raised my right hand as instructed, and as I did, I could see Clyde out of the corner of my eye, staring at me. After we were all sworn in, I reclaimed my seat as I listened to the bailiff announce our case. I could still feel Clyde staring at me. What was his deal?

"I have reviewed all of the evidence submitted by both parties, and I am ready to render my decision," Judge Elliott said.

I took a deep breath and glanced over at Clyde who had leaned over and was whispering something in his lawyer's ear.

Clyde's lawyer, in turn, jumped up from his seat and said, "I apologize, Your Honor, but my client would like to make a request of the court."

The judge frowned. "Can this not wait until after I'm done? Is this request pertinent to the case?"

"Um, Your Honor, Mr. Morgan would like to speak with his wife before we proceed," Clyde's lawyer said.

The judge sighed and then turned toward my table. "Ms. Mixon, does Ms. Brooks have any objections?"

Shelly looked at me, awaiting my answer. I looked back at Reggie who wore a confused look on his face and then over at Clyde, who gave me a weak smile. I returned my gaze to Shelly.

"It's okay," I whispered with a nod. Although part of me despised Clyde, another part of me wanted to hear what he had to say.

"Your Honor, my client has no objections," Shelly said.

Judge Elliott nodded. "Very well. We will recess and promptly reconvene in an hour," she said with a bang of the gavel.

Shelly leaned close to me and whispered, "I hope you know what you're doing, and I certainly hope this hasn't been a waste of my time."

I shook my head. "Nothing's changed. He wants to talk, and I'm willing to listen. That's all."

Shelly gave me a skeptical look as I stood up and grabbed my purse. Clyde walked over to me with a sheepish look on his face.

"So, uh you wanna go and get a cup of coffee? There's a place right across the street," Clyde said.

I nodded. "Sure, but can you give me a minute?"

Clyde nodded and I quickly made my way over to Reggie. He was visibly upset and before I could speak, he held his hand up to silence me.

"It's okay. Go talk to him." He said then looked away from me and shoved his hands in the pockets of his slacks.

"Talk is all we're gonna do, Reggie. I promise," I said.

"Yeah. Go ahead," Reggie replied sounding less than convinced.

I looked up at him and hesitated for a moment before exiting the courtroom with Clyde.

♫♫♫

I nervously tapped my foot and traced the rim of my cup with my finger as I awaited Clyde's return to the small café table. We had made the short walk across the street from the courthouse to the coffee shop together in silence.

I'd been the first to order, and as I nursed my caramel dream cappuccino, Clyde stood at the counter and customized his black coffee with cream and sugar. Finally finished, he made his way to the table and took a seat across from me. He took a sip and then smiled at me.

"Bobbie, you look good, *real good*," he said and then took another sip of his coffee.

I glanced down at the black pants and white ruffled blouse I wore. "Um, thanks."

"Yeah, you look like you've been taking real good care of yourself, resting."

"Thanks." I looked down at my cup. "You wanted to talk, Clyde?"

Clyde cleared his throat. "Yeah, um I wanted to tell you that I'm sorry for how things went down between us, you know?"

I twisted my mouth, furrowed my brow, and said, "How things went down?"

He looked down at his cup. "Yeah, you know. How I left things."

I nodded and widened my eyes. "Oh, you mean how you left me without a word or a dime during my tour, cancelled my credit cards, and cleaned out the closet *and* the bank accounts without so much as a goodbye? You mean how all of *that* went down?" I said angrily.

He shifted his eyes. "Um yeah, that. I'm sorry about that, but I guess I figured you'd be okay. You know, with your work and all."

"With my work, huh? I see. Go on." I took a sip of my coffee and fought the desire to dash it on him and ruin his nice suit.

"Um, I realize now that you're the best thing that ever happened to me." He paused and then reached across the table and grasped my hand. "I messed up bad. I miss you, little girl. I miss you a lot, and I love you."

"Really?" I asked, actually shocked at his declaration.

"Yeah, I miss taking care of you."

I nodded and looked down at our joined hands. I thought about all of the sleepless nights during which I'd wished for this moment. How I'd longed to hear the words he spoke. Was he serious or was he just playing some kind of game with me?

"And I wanna stop the divorce. We can try again. Make things right," he said.

I sat silently for a moment and then said, "What about Sabrina?"

He dropped his eyes. "Ain't no more Sabrina. It didn't work out between us."

"Oh really, what happened?"

He looked up at me. "Hell, little girl, she wasn't you. Baby, you the only one for me. I realize that now, and I'm sorry."

I closed my eyes. I had to admit that I did miss Clyde in a lot of ways. I mean, when things between us were good, they were *very good*.

"Clyde, you know you really hurt me. You hurt me bad," I said.

He nodded vigorously. "I know, I know and I'm sorry. I'll do anything to make it up to you. *Anything*. Just give me a chance, little girl. I just want my beautiful wife back."

I leaned back in my chair and thought about what he'd said. "Um, Clyde, can you excuse me for a moment?" I asked.

"Yeah, I'll be right here," Clyde replied.

I left the table and went to the small ladies room located at the rear of the tiny restaurant. I closed myself inside a stall, pulled my cell phone out of my purse, and then dialed the number.

"Hello," Reggie answered in the middle of the first ring, sounding anxious.

"Reg, it's Bobbie," I said.

"I know."

"Did you really mean what you said to me the other week?"

"About what?"

"That you'd wait for me."

"Of course I meant it. I love you, Bobbie Ann."

"You'll wait no matter how long it takes for me to say yes?"

"That's right. Why?"

"I just needed to know. I'll talk to you later, okay?"

"Okay. I love you."

I hung up and returned to the table. Clyde looked up at me with a curious expression as I took my seat.

"Okay Clyde, do you really mean what you've been saying?"

He gave me a sincere look. "Yeah, I really do."

"Okay. And you really wanna make things right with me?"

He nodded. "Yeah, just tell me what you want."

I took a deep breath and then began to speak. First I apologized for my role in the breakdown of our marriage. Then, we continued to talk and near the end of the hour, we had come to an agreement. I re-entered the courtroom with a smile and then quickly filled Shelly in on what we had decided. She jotted down some notes on a pad and nodded as I spoke. Shortly thereafter, everyone in the room rose as Judge Elliott made her entrance.

# TWENTY

### "Blues Power"

"MR. Martin, is your client ready to proceed?" Judge Elliott asked, peering over her glasses at Clyde's lawyer.

"Um, Your Honor, it seems that Mr. Morgan and Ms. Brooks have reached an agreement of their own and would like the court's approval," Clyde's lawyer replied.

The judge nodded. "Okay, let's hear it."

"Mr. Morgan has agreed to forego the petition for spousal maintenance, choosing instead to receive his standard 30% manager's fee from any royalties Ms. Brooks receives for work performed during the marriage. Mr. Morgan and Ms. Brooks have agreed to retain their own vehicles. Ms. Brooks will retain the primary residence, the townhouse located here in Dallas, and Mr. Morgan will retain the home in Houston. All other property will be sold and the proceeds will be split 50/50. Mr. Morgan's stake in his business ventures will be liquidated and those funds will be split equally as well. The couple has also agreed to evenly split the proceeds in each of their bank accounts."

"Sounds reasonable." Judge Elliott actually sounded rather surprised. "Ms. Mixon, Ms. Brooks agrees to these terms?"

Shelly nodded. "Yes, Your Honor."

"Very well. It is so ordered. It's good to see two adults able to settle their differences and behave maturely. Court is adjourned."

I breathed a sigh of relief then turned and smiled at Clyde. I thanked Shelly and made my way to Reggie, who greeted me with open arms. I laid my head on his chest as he hugged me.

"Aw man, Bobbie, you had me scared there for a minute," he whispered into my ear.

"Scared of what?" I asked.

"Of losing you to him," he said as he nodded towards Clyde.

"Ah, you got me, Reverend Darrough. I might not be the best decision-maker in the world, but there's no way I'm trading you in for Clyde."

"That's good to know." He released me and with bright smile said, "I tell you what. Let's celebrate your new-found freedom."

I laughed. "I'd love to, and I know some great places here. We could spend the night."

He shook his head. "Naw, I know of a place back home. I think you'll like it."

I shrugged. "Okay, fine with me."

"Okay, let's head back. We can have dinner with Mama and then head out if that's okay with you. I need to check on her."

"That's fine. Do I need to change?"

"Unh uh, you look perfect."

♫♫♫

After we had a rather healthy dinner of baked chicken, green salad, and steamed vegetables, prepared by a hired cook, we sat and chatted with Ms. Cassie. Upon our arrival, she'd greeted me with open arms and a knowing smile and when Reggie excused himself to go to the bathroom; she'd told me how happy she was to see us together again.

"Thank you for making my boy so happy. That Caprice had really broken him down, but now he's back to his old self," she'd said.

I shook my head. "No ma'am. I didn't do anything. Reggie's been so good to me. I'm the one who's thankful. He's a wonderful man."

Ms. Cassie leaned forward in the recliner. Dressed in a faded pink duster and worn blue house shoes, she looked like a short, round cream puff.

"Well," she said, "he loves you, and evidently, loving you makes him happy. So thank you for lettin' him love you."

I smiled. "I love him, too." I said it before I realized it, but I guess it was true. I did love him.

Reggie entered the room as if on cue and bent over and kissed his mother on the cheek. She was several shades lighter-skinned than Reggie with freckles sprinkled over her cheeks. I'd heard that her father was a white man and looking at her face to face, I believed it to be true. She and Reggie shared the same wide-set hazel eyes, the same medium wide nose, and the same curly hair although her sandy hair was mangled with gray and Reggie's was jet black. Reggie's full lips and brown skin as well as his tall stature must have come directly from his father, a man who he'd only seen a handful of times in his life.

"Mama, you gonna be alright? You need anything before we go?" He asked.

"Boy, I'll be fine. I'm not an invalid. You and Bobbie Ann go and have a good time." Ms. Cassie answered.

"You sure?" Reggie queried.

"Reggie, y'all go on." Ms. Cassie looked over at me. "Take him, please."

I laughed. "Yes, ma'am."

Reggie kissed his mother's cheek again and then walked over to me and took my hand.

"Okay, bye Mama," Reggie said.

Ms. Cassie waved. "Bye. Y'all have a good time."

♫♫♫

Reggie drove for about 30 minutes before finally arriving at a small, cinder block building.

"Where are we?" I asked.

"Prescott," he said.

I smiled. "This looks like one of those little juke joints my daddy used to take me to perform in way back."

"It might be one of them. This is Riley's Place."

"What?! I think I performed here when I was like 15."

He smiled and nodded. "Yeah, I remember you telling me something about this place."

Reggie walked around to the passenger's side and opened the door for me. Hand in hand, we walked into the small space which was pretty packed for a Thursday night. Reggie led me to a table near the back of the club and as I took my seat, he left to get us a couple of sodas.

I settled into my seat and looked around the room, which had not changed much in 15 years. There was a small bar which was trimmed in brown vinyl and boasted a mirrored wall behind it. The round bar stools looked as if their matching brown vinyl cushions were in bad need of an upholsterer's attention. The dark wood paneled walls were covered with worn and faded photos of blues and soul artists, including myself. I smiled faintly at the old photo of me as a 20-year-old singer, wearing a tight red dress and red heels to match my bright red lipstick. My hair was fashioned in huge braids.

There was only room in the place for a small bandstand and a microscopic dance floor which consisted of scuffed-up black linoleum. In addition, there were about twenty square tables with faux wooden tops and wooden t-style legs. The black vinyl-backed and seated chairs were uncomfortable to say the least, but I had a sneaking suspicion that after a few drinks, no one complained about them.

Reggie returned with our sodas and said, "Anything look familiar?"

"Yeah," I said, "this place hasn't changed a bit. I bet they still sell barbecue sandwiches in the back."

Reggie grinned and nodded. "Yeah and according to the bartender, they sell fish plates, too. Complete with onion slices, pickle spear, and hot sauce on the side."

I smiled and threw my head back. "Aw, it's good to be back in Arkansas where the folks know how to *throw down* with the food!"

Reggie laughed. "Yeah, I know right? Italy is a great place to eat, but you can't beat some good ol' southern soul food."

We sat and listened to the music, danced to a few songs, and ate a couple of the best barbecue sandwiches I've ever had. Full of food and soda, we hit the tiny dance floor for a couple more songs. After a quick trip to the restroom, I returned to our table, Reggie, and a fresh soda.

I leaned close to him and tried to speak above the music. "You know, this is the most fun I've had in a while, but it feels kinda strange, too."

He frowned. "Why strange?"

"Well, I haven't been sober in a club in years. It feels good, though, real good."

"Good. I'm glad, Bobbie."

At that moment, the DJ began to speak into the microphone from the small booth in the corner of the room. "Ladies and gents, we got a bonafide star in the house tonight. In our midst is none other than one of Arkansas' own, Ms. Bobbie BluAnn Brooks."

A soft murmur spread across the crowd as I bucked my eyes and looked over at Reggie.

He shook his head and held his hands up. "I didn't say a word."

I glared at him.

"Come on, Bobbie. You're a blues star, and we're in a blues club. You couldn't have thought you could go the whole night unnoticed. I mean, they've played three of your songs since we've been here, and people have been staring over here all night."

"Yeah, I know." I said under my breath. I stood, flashed my best smile, and waved at the crowd.

"Don't y'all wanna hear this lovely lady sing tonight?" the DJ asked.

The crowd applauded and several people shouted, "Yeah!"

I sat back down and leaned closer to Reggie. "I'm scared. It's been a long time since I performed sober, too. I don't know if I can do it," I whispered.

He raised his eyebrows. "Bobbie, God gave you that voice and nothing can take it from you. Besides, unless you plan on retiring now, you better get in some practice."

I nodded. He was definitely right. I sat there for a few seconds, took a deep breath, and then made my way to the stage. I stepped onto the small platform and whispered the name of one of my older songs to the keyboardist, who along with a guitarist and drummer, made up the house band.

I took the microphone off its stand and said, "It's good to be back at Riley's. It's been a long time. I'mma sing an oldie for y'all. I hope y'all enjoy it."

I nodded my head to the beat as the musicians began to play "All Yours", a mid-tempo song that had always been really popular in Arkansas. The crowd, who appeared to instantly recognize the song, stood from their seats and began to dance to the music. I smiled as I began to sing the lyrics:

*"Boy, you know you got me where you want me
Can't let go, you're the only place I wanna be*

*Love's so good, it feels just like a fantasy
It's understood, how good your body feels to me*

*Baby don't worry, if ever there's any doubt
Cause anytime you touch me, you turn me inside out*

*It's yours
Baby, all yours
From sun up to sun down
It's all yours
No matter what you do or say
No matter the time of day
My lovin', my lovin' is all yours..."*

I sang and rocked and teased until the song was over. I grinned as the crowd sang and danced along with me, and once I was finished, I felt pretty good about the short performance. I bowed, thanked the crowd, and then navigated my way back to Reggie. As I took my seat, I wiped my brow with a napkin.

Reggie grinned and shook his head. "You are something else, Bobbie Brooks."

I took a sip of my soda and said, "Yeah, well what you think of me now that you've seen first-hand what I *really* do for a living? You still wanna marry me, Reggie Darrough?"

Reggie leaned across the table and planted a long, slow kiss on my lips.

After our lips had parted, I said, "My my my, what would the church folk have to say about you sitting up in a nightclub kissing on a blues singer, Rev. Darrough?"

He raised his eyebrows. "I really don't care. I don't have to answer to anyone but God, my dear."

"And what would *He* say?"

"That there's nothing wrong with love, and I certainly love you, Superstar."

"I love you, too."

# TWENTY-ONE

### "Confessing the Blues"

I walked into Dr. Barlow's inner office for what was to be my last prescribed session and smiled as I took my seat.

She returned my smile and said, "How are you feeling today, Bobbie?"

"Pretty good. No, great actually," I replied.

She nodded and raised her eyebrows. "And your day in court?"

"It went pretty well. Clyde really surprised me." I proceeded to fill her in on our conversation and subsequent agreement.

"Well, do you think the two of you came to the best decision?"

I nodded. "I think so. I mean 30% is a ridiculous fee for a manager, but he was more than that. He was basically my caregiver, so I think I probably owe him that much for the work we did together."

"I see. So where do you go from here?"

I shrugged. "Well, I plan to continue with the AA meetings even when I get back to Dallas. Those meetings keep me focused on what

I need to do to stay sober."

She nodded. "Okay."

"And I think I'm ready for a future with Reggie, after I've told him everything, of course."

"Are you ready to tell him now?"

I sighed and nodded my head. "I believe I'm as ready as I'll ever be."

"Even at the risk of hurting him?"

I dropped my eyes. "Yes and even at the risk of losing him."

"Do you believe that he really loves you, Bobbie?"

I smiled. "I know he does. I have no doubt about that, and I love him, too."

"Then why would you fear losing him?"

"I don't know. I guess I'm really underestimating him. He's a good man and a forgiving person. I'm gonna tell him and then let the chips fall where they may."

Dr. Barlow smiled. "Bobbie, I have a feeling that you're strong enough to handle whatever comes your way."

I nodded. "You know, for the first time in my life, I feel the same way."

♫♫♫

I closed my eyes and laid my head back against the plush seat of Reggie's SUV. It was a crisp Thursday evening in late November and we were on our way to my weekly AA meeting. Right at that moment, I was feeling pretty happy.

"You tired?" Reggie asked, then reached over and rubbed my hand.

I smiled, my eyes still closed. "Not really, just feeling relaxed and at peace. Like no matter what happens, everything'll be okay." I opened my eyes and looked over at Reggie.

He glanced at me and smiled. His eyes were simply beautiful as he nodded. "It *will* be. I'll make sure of it."

"You really mean that?" I asked softly.

He flashed me a sincere look. "Yeah, I really do."

"Reggie, I did some really crazy stuff in my past. Things I'm not proud of."

He shrugged. "So did I."

I reached over and rubbed his arm. "Pull over."

His expression changed to one of confusion. "We're only a couple of minutes from the church."

"I know. Just pull over."

Reggie pulled his vehicle to a stop on the parking lot of a local school. "What's wrong?"

I sat up in my seat. "Nothing." I reached for his hand. "Reggie, do you remember when we were kids growing up?"

He nodded. "Yeah."

"I had this huge crush on you for years."

"You did?"

"Yeah, I did. I was crazy about you long before you paid any attention to me."

He frowned. "I'm sorry, I didn't know."

I shook my head. "Just listen. When we finally got together, I was so happy. It was just like I'd imagined it would be, a dream come true. You were so kind, so good to me; just like now."

He stared at me, but remained quiet.

"You made me feel so safe. You still do, and I love you for it. I love you so much, Reg."

"I love you, too."

I smiled. "I know you do. Now, lemme see your keys."

"What? Why?"

Without another word, I reached over and took his keys out of the ignition and then unlocked the glove compartment. Reggie's eyes widened as I pulled the black ring box out and opened it.

"What are you doing?" he asked, now thoroughly confused.

I leaned over the center console and slowly, softly kissed him on his lips. As we parted, I removed the ring from the box and handed it to him.

"Put it on my finger," I said.

Reggie's eyes searched mine and as he lowered them to look at the ring, I could see tears begin to form. "Does this mean that—"

I placed a finger against his lips. "Shh. Just put it on my finger."

He stared at me for a moment and then obliged me by sliding the gorgeous piece of jewelry onto my left ring finger. I smiled as I rubbed my finger across the princess-cut diamond.

"Yes," I said.

"Yes?" He repeated. He sounded surprised.

"Yes, I'll marry you."

"You will?"

I nodded. "I will."

Reggie opened his door and slid out of the vehicle. I watched as he hurriedly walked around the front of the truck and then opened my door. He grabbed my hand, pulling me out of the vehicle and into his arms. He held me so close to him that I could feel his heartbeat. I closed my eyes as he leaned over and kissed me with a full measure of both love and passion. I wrapped my arms around him and surrendered to his touch. After several minutes, he released me. I looked up at him and saw that his face was wet with tears.

"You'll never regret this, I promise," he said.

I reached up and wiped his face with my fingers. "Neither will you. I love you, Reggie, and I always will."

He held me close and kissed my forehead. I smiled, and at that moment, I felt like the luckiest woman in the world. A few minutes later, we'd both climbed back into the truck and had made it to the church parking lot.

I looked down at the ring on my finger, then up at Reggie. "There's something I need to tell you, after the meeting. Something really important."

He leaned over and kissed me. "Okay."

He walked me to the fellowship hall and hugged me. "I love you," he whispered in my ear.

"I love you, too," I replied. And I really did.

♫♫♫

"Well, brothers and sisters, we're up to step 12. I don't have anyone scheduled to speak tonight, so I'll just open the floor to you guys. I'm not gonna hog the mic." Rev. Lee paused as the group erupted in laughter. "If anyone has something to share, the floor is yours."

I looked around the room and then nervously and slowly raised my hand. Lee's head snapped in my direction.

"Yes! Bobbie, do you have something to share?" He asked.

I stood, rubbed my hands on my blue jeans, and made my way to the podium. Lee smiled at me and adjusted the mic to a height comfortable for me.

I glanced around the room, cleared my throat, and began to speak. "Um, hello everyone, I'm Bobbie, and I'm an alcoholic." I smiled as the crowd sang a chorus of "Hello Bobbie".

I took a deep breath and continued. "Um, you guys'll have to forgive me because I'm pretty nervous, which is odd because I've spent most of my life on a stage and in front of huge crowds.

"Well first, I wanna thank you all for sharing your stories. You've all been an inspiration to me. Um, I feel like I've been kinda selfish though, sitting in here week after week listening and learning. Taking and not giving, so tonight it's my turn to tell my story.

"For several years, I've lived life as a functional alcoholic. I used alcohol to give me the courage to step onto the stage and sing love songs when I felt unloved and to sing sad songs that hit a little too close to home. I drank when I was stressed or sad. I drank to mask the pain of a failed marriage, the loss of my dear father, and the strained relationship with my mother. But most of all…" I paused as my voice began to break and blinked back tears, and then I continued.

"Most of all, I drank to forget what I did one November day, several years ago. I was 18-years-old and back then, I was in love with this tall, handsome boy and he loved me, too. We were inseparable and had made so many plans for the future. He was a year older than me and by then had left for college on a basketball scholarship.

"Like most young men from small towns, he got caught up in the excitement and popularity of being a college basketball star. He lost touch with me so he had no way of knowing that I was three months pregnant with his child. He didn't know I was scared and alone. To top it all off, I'd just been offered my first record deal. I couldn't hear from him, and I was desperate to succeed as a performer because it had been my dream since I was a little girl.

"So I took some of the money I'd saved up from performing at small clubs and blues festivals down through the years and took a bus to Little Rock. Um, I went to this clinic and I …I," I paused and wiped the tears from my face with the sleeve of my shirt. Lee handed me a tissue.

I released a ragged sigh and then continued to speak. "I had an abortion and the very thought of it has haunted me every day since.

I've hated myself for doing it, and I never forgave myself. I don't even think I can get pregnant anymore. I tried for years to have a baby with my husband and couldn't. For awhile I felt like I was being punished, but I've done a lot of praying and soul searching, and I know that God has forgiven me. I finally forgive myself, too. So I guess what I want you to know is that everything I've learned here is true, and it really works if you try it. I thank you guys for your fellowship, but most of all, I thank Jesus for saving me from myself."

I offered the crowd a weak smile and walked back to my seat amidst their applause, my vision blurred with tears. Several people, some whom I'd actually grown pretty close to, hugged me as I passed by them. I finally made it to my seat and as I turned to sit down, I noticed Reggie standing in the back of the room with a stricken look on his face. In his hand, he held a bouquet of flowers. My heart fell.

# TWENTY-TWO

### "Baby, Please Don't Go"

REGGIE backed out of the door. I grabbed my purse and quickly exited the fellowship hall behind him.

"Reggie!" I called after him as he strode across the parking lot.

"Reggie, please wait!" I pleaded.

Reggie spun on his heels and glared at me. "What Bobbie?" he grunted. "What could you possibly have to say to me?"

I'd finally caught up with him and stood before him trying to catch my breath. "I...I'm sorry. I didn't know you were in there." I reached for him and he backed away from me.

"What's that supposed to mean? If you'd known I was there, you wouldn't have told it? Is that what you're saying, Bobbie Ann?"

I shook my head. "No, I mean, I didn't want you to find out like this. I was gonna tell you tonight, after the meeting. I really was."

"Twelve years, Bobbie. *Twelve years* and you were gonna tell me *tonight* and only *after* you told a room full of strangers?!"

"They're not strangers to me anymore, Reggie. They're more like family to me now."

"But are they me, Bobbie? *I* was that baby's father! I shoulda been the first to know! You did it without even discussing it with me. I had a right to know!" He yelled.

I looked around at the empty parking lot and then turned back to Reggie. His pain was written all over his face and inside, I was literally dying.

"Reggie, I wanted to tell you. I tried, I really did. I just, I was so scared. I didn't wanna hurt you, but that's exactly what I did. I'm so, so sorry." Tears began to pour from my eyes as I clutched my gut. I was beginning to feel nauseated.

He shook his head in disgust. "All I ever wanted to do was to make things right between us. I just wanted to love you, Bobbie. That's it. It's all I've thought about, all I've dreamed about. Even when I was married, I thought about you all the time. You were it for me." He paused as his voice began to break. "Why didn't you just tell me? I would've come home and taken care of both of you. You didn't have to do it."

I nodded through my tears. "I know that now, but I was young and scared, and I didn't have anyone to talk to. I didn't know what else to do. I mean, you had your dreams and I had mine. I just didn't wanna mess things up."

"Mess things up?! That was our child, Bobbie, a gift from God. How could a child mess things up?"

I shook my head. "You say that now, but back then, would you have seen things the same way? I thought you'd be angry with me for ruining your future, your life."

Reggie leaned against his truck and shook his head. "You didn't make the baby by yourself, Bobbie. What right would I have had to be angry with you?"

"I don't know. That's just how I felt. That's what I was afraid of. I was young, and I was alone."

"Yeah well, you should've told me and given me the benefit of the doubt."

"Well, I never thought you would've lost touch with me, but you did. I guess I felt like you deserted me," I said quietly.

Reggie shook his head and laughed bitterly. "Yeah well, I guess there's nothing predictable about either one of us. But you know what, Bobbie ? I think in twelve years you coulda found a way to tell me. But you didn't, did you? You just went about your life like nothing happened. I would never think you could be so cold and heartless."

The tears continued to fall from my eyes. I wiped my cheek. "I don't know, Reggie. I guess I blocked it out. It was too painful."

"Wow, and I thought that I couldn't even make a baby. After my wife seemed to be able get pregnant by everyone *but* me, I just figured I was sterile or something. But it actually turns out that I *can* make babies and I did make one, but…"

"Reggie, please listen to me. I am so sorry. I mean that from the bottom of my heart. Please don't hate me." I placed my hand on his arm.

He dropped his head. "I just wanted a family, that's all. That's all I've ever wanted. I didn't realize that I was asking for so much."

"Oh God, Reggie. Please forgive me. We can make a family together. We can still make it work."

Reggie looked at me, his face wet with tears. "What's so wrong with me, Bobbie?"

I frowned and said, "Nothing! It was my fault, and I'm sorry. I shoulda told you, no matter how mad I thought you would get. You had a right to know."

Reggie shook his head and buried his face in his hands. I reached up and moved his hands and then fell against his chest and hugged him tightly. We stood there next to his SUV and cried together until we heard the other AA participants filing out of the building. Reggie finally released me and wiped his eyes with the sleeve of his jacket. He picked up the bouquet he'd laid on the hood of his vehicle and handed it to me.

"I better get you home," he said, without looking me in the eye and then walked around and opened my door for me.

I climbed in and after he'd settled into the driver's seat and started the truck, I said, "Reggie, are you sure you're okay to drive?"

He sniffed then nodded. "Yeah, I'm fine," he said softly.

"Reggie, I'm really sorry."

He shook his head and looked me in the eye. It nearly killed me to see the pain in his eyes.

"No need to be," he said.

The ride to my mom's house was spent in silence. I stared out at the darkness as Reggie drove, his hands tightly gripping the wheel. I wanted to apologize and ask for forgiveness over and over again, but sensed that it would be best to just keep quiet.

Reggie pulled up to my mother's house and parked in the driveway after what felt like a painfully endless ride. He climbed out of the vehicle and opened the door for me, giving me his hand to hold onto as I stepped out onto the ground.

"Reggie, I hope you can forgive me," I said softly.

"I already have," he said, but did not look me in the eye.

I stood on my toes and kissed him softly on the lips. Once our lips had parted, I stepped back and looked up at him. He stood still and stared at me with no expression on his face.

"I love you, Reggie," I said, barely above a whisper.

Finally he nodded, then took my left hand and rubbed his fingers across my ring. "I love you, too. Goodnight, Bobbie Ann," he said.

Reggie walked me to the door and then kissed me, this time on my forehead. I walked inside the house and climbed into bed. I wondered why his "goodnight" had felt like a "goodbye". I closed my eyes and said a silent prayer before crying myself to sleep.

♫♫♫

The next morning there was no call from Reggie. I tried to reach him several times but every call went straight to voicemail. I left message after message but received no return phone call. I was upset, but I went about my daily routine as best I could. The thing is that talking to or seeing Reggie had become a big part of that routine, and I already missed him.

I quietly cleaned the house, ate lunch, watched TV, made a few calls to both my manager and accountant, sat on the porch, fixed dinner, and finally went to bed. The entire day passed by without a word from Reggie.

Saturday brought more of the same. When Sunday arrived, I thought that at least I'd see him at church, but I was mistaken. As I sat next to Mama and the girls, I watched the preachers file into the sanctuary. Reggie was nowhere to be found. I was really beginning to worry about him. I knew that he was upset with me to say the least, but it was not like him at all to miss church. Not at all.

As the church prayed together, I prayed for Reggie, hoping that neither he nor his mother was ill. I also prayed for myself because, I loved him, and I was hurting. I don't think that I fully realized just how much Reggie meant to me until I realized that there was a chance I'd lose him.

A few more days passed by, and I was still unable to reach Reggie. Finally, on the day of my next AA meeting, I called his mother. I just needed to know what was going on.

"Hello," Ms. Cassie answered.

"Ms. Cassie, its Bobbie Ann. H…how are you?" I said.

"Hey baby, well I'm doin' tolerable well. How you?"

"Um, I'm ok. Is…is Reggie home?"

"Well, didn't he tell you?"

I frowned at her question. "Tell me what?"

"Baby, he left and went back to Italy. He still got a house over there, you know."

"W…what? When did he leave?"

"Last Sunday mornin'. Say he needed to take care of some business. Not sho' when he'll be back."

I blinked back tears and said, "Oh, okay. Um, if you hear from him, will you ask him to call me?"

"Sho' will. He calls me every day."

"Okay, thank you, Ms. Cassie."

"You welcome, baby. Tell yo' mama I said hi."

"I will."

I ended the call and collapsed across my bed in tears. I knew that the only business Reggie was taking care of was the business of forgetting about me. I'd messed up the best thing that had ever happened to me, and there was nothing I could do about it. I felt like my heart had been ripped out of my chest. I lay in that bed and cried until I ran out of tears.

To be honest, that was the first time in a long while that I really felt like I needed a drink. I shut my eyes and prayed hard. It was all I could do not to set out walking to a liquor store or the local bootlegger's house and pick up a bottle of anything brown and fermented that they had on hand. So, afraid I would do just that, I laid there in that bed and did not move. I was still laying there when Mama and the girls made it home.

Mama walked quietly into my bedroom and said, "Bobbie Ann, you feelin' okay? What you doin' in da bed dis time uh day?"

I quickly sat up, wiped my tear-streaked face, and rubbed my hand through my hair. The last thing I needed at that point was to hear any of her fussing.

"I'm okay. Lemme go get started on dinner. I'm sorry, I'm running a little behind schedule today," I said, then lowered my head and tried to walk past her, but she stopped me.

Mama placed her hand on my chest and said, "Unh uh Bobbie Ann, you can't fool me. What's da matter witchu?"

I sighed and shook my head. "Mama, you wouldn't understand."

She frowned. "How you know if you don't tell me?"

I leaned against the bed. "Reggie and me broke up." It was all I could do not to cry as I said the words.

Her eyes widened. "But you still wearin' his ring," she said and pointed at my left hand.

I looked down at my hand. "Yeah, well I guess he was too mad at me to even bother taking it back. He just up and left for Italy. He didn't even tell me he was going."

"Italy?! What happened?"

I shifted my eyes. "Um, he found out about something that happened when we were kids, and it hurt him, so he left. It's…it's over between us."

She shut the door to my bedroom then lowered her voice and asked, "He found out 'bout da abortion?"

My head snapped up and I looked at her in shock. "Y…you knew?"

"Of course I knew. I could tell you was expectin'. Yo' body had done started ta change. And den dat day you said you was auditionin' for a job, you came back here all out of it. You bled so much you messed up yo sheets. I knew what you had did."

I wiped the tears that rolled down my cheeks. "Did Daddy know?"

"You mean did I tell 'em? Naw, I didn't. It woulda killed him if he knew. You was his princess."

"All these years you knew? I can't believe it. Why didn't you say something?" I said.

She put her hands on her hips and said, "What was I 'spose to say, Bobbie Ann?"

I gave her a desperate look. "I don't know. Maybe something motherly, like 'it'll be okay'. I guess it woulda helped for me to know that someone else knew. I always felt so alone with this."

"Well, I didn't think it was none uh my business. You was a grown woman."

I bucked my eyes at her. "Mama, I was *eighteen*! Being eighteen doesn't make you a grown person!"

Mama shrugged. "I didn't figure you needed me. You never needed me befoe'."

I frowned. "What?! What are you talking about? You're my *mother*! Of course I needed you."

"Yeah, but it was always just you and yo' daddy. I never fit wit y'all."

"Fit? I needed a mother *and* a father. I needed for *you* to be my mother. Do you know how I've felt all these years? How empty I felt because I thought I'd done something to make you hate me?"

It was Mama's turn to frown. "Hate you? Bobbie Ann, I love you. I always have. I jus' thought you didn't need me. Dat's all."

"But how could you think that? I was just a little girl. You must've known that I needed my mother."

Mama stood there silently as I dissolved into tears. She stood there for several minutes and stared at me, then finally reached over and patted my shoulder. It was an awkward attempt at comforting me, but at least she was trying.

"Well, I'm sorry, Bobbie Ann. I didn't know you felt dat way. I jus' always figured you didn't want me involved in yo' life."

I shook my head. "Mama, I just wanted you to love me but I never felt like you did. You never told me or showed me."

"Well, I did love you, and I still do." She folded her arms across her chest and sighed. "All dis time I thought it was yo' daddy and da blues what messed you up, but I guess it was me. I was so jealous uh how close you and yo' daddy was, I forgot ta be yo' mama."

I looked up at her. "You think I'm a bad person for what I did? For what I did to my baby?"

She shook her head. "I think you was afraid and confused, and you did what you thought was right. Now, you know better, and when you know better, you do better. Anyway, I know jus' how ya felt."

I gave her a confused look. "How could you possibly know? You had Daddy. He was always there for you."

Mama sighed. "Bobbie Ann, there's a lot you don't know about me. A lot I been through."

I sniffed. "Like what?"

She looked me in the eye. "Like yo' daddy ain't Junior's daddy."

"What?!"

"I was already pregnant by somebody else when we started courtin'."

"You were what?!" Was she for real?

She nodded and said, "I was pregnant by Delma Dansby."

"Who?" I asked with a wrinkled brow.

"He was the star of the basketball team, and I had this big crush on him."

"He was your boyfriend?"

"Naw, not hardly. He wadnt thinkin' 'bout me like that."

"Well, then how'd you—"

"He raped me."

I held my hand to my mouth. "What?! Oh, Mama. I'm so sorry."

She held her hand up and shook her head. "It's alright. I was young and silly, and I liked him. I liked him too much, I guess. I let 'em take advantage of me. He offered ta walk me home from school one day, and I let him, thinkin' dat he liked me, too. He got me down da road from my house and pushed me in da woods and dat's where he raped me. Den I came up pregnant."

I shook my head. "Oh Mama, you must've been scared to death."

Mama leaned against the bed. "Ta death is right! Thangs was different back den, especially 'round here. You was looked down on real bad for gettin' pregnant outta wedlock. I was too scared ta tell my mama or anybody. I didn't think nobody would believe I was raped."

"How did you end up with Daddy?"

"I already knew yo' daddy. Grew up wit' 'em. He always had a crush on me and would hang around me all da time, but I wouldn't pay no 'tention to 'em. Well, one day, I guess I was 'bout a month along. Yo' daddy saw me sittin' on the front porch cryin' and asked me what was wrong. I told 'em 'bout Delma and da baby and he—" She stopped and shook her head. I think she was actually about to cry. That was the most emotion my mother had ever shown in front of me.

"He said he'd take care of me and da baby. Said he'd raise it as his own. He wadnt but nineteen hisself, but he got a job, and we got married. He was da one what wanted ta name da baby Earl Jr."

"I never would've known that Junior wasn't his. I even thought Junior kinda looked like Daddy."

Mama smiled. "Yeah, he kinda do, don't he?"

I nodded. "I'm sorry, Mama. I didn't realize you'd been through all of that."

"Yeah, well if it hadn't been fo' yo' daddy, I mighta been in da same situation as you. So what I'm tryna say is dat I understand how you felt and what you went through. You was jus' young and scared and alone."

At hearing her last statement, I totally broke down. Mama wrapped her arms around me and gave me the first hug I can ever remember receiving from her. I rested my head on her shoulder and cried for what felt like hours. Finally, Mama let me go, stepped back and raised my chin with her hand.

"Listen to me, Bobbie Ann. Reggie's a good man, just like yo' daddy. He probably more upset wit' hisself than anyone else. He upset wit' hisself for not being there for ya when you needed him. He'll be back. Don't chu worry."

"I just don't know, Mama. He was really hurt."

She smiled. "He loves you, and he'll be back. Dat much I know fo' sho'. Take it from an old hen. I know."

I wiped my wet face, and I hoped and prayed that Mama was right.

# TWENTY-THREE

### "Waiting For Your Call"

I rolled down the window on my truck and smiled as the unseasonably warm January air hit my face and blew through my hair. It was perfect t-shirt and blue jean weather, and the citizens of Dallas were out taking full advantage of it. As I drove down Don Drive, I smiled at the couples holding hands and walking down the sidewalk. I, myself, had had a great day in the studio and was looking forward to relaxing at home with a long, hot bath.

I'd left Mama's house right after Christmas and had returned to Dallas, my townhouse, and my music. I was really feeling pretty good about myself and my life. No, I still hadn't heard from Reggie, nor had I seen him since before he left for Italy. I missed him more than I could have ever imagined. I thought about him all the time and wrote tons of songs about him. I still wore his ring, and I still held onto hope that we'd get back together, eventually. I loved Reggie, and it made me sad to think about how I'd hurt him. I prayed that he'd find a way to heal just as I finally had. I prayed that he would one day forgive me.

I kept in touch with Mama and actually had real conversations with her. We laughed and talked, and she kept me up-to-date on the happenings in Willisville. We got along really well, now. Opening up to one another had allowed our relationship to grow. Knowing everything Mama had been through in her life had shed new light on the way she raised me. She'd endured so much heartache and pain that she'd emotionally detached herself from most everyone, especially me. I understood her now and accepted her for who she was.

Meka and Sharee were still behaving and my brother Junior and their mother, Nora Lee, were still absent. Sometimes, I wondered if they were even still alive. Whatever the case with them was, I never forgot them in my prayers.

I halted my thoughts and parked my car in my driveway. I headed into my house and once inside, dropped my keys on the pedestal table in the foyer, and then sifted through the day's mail. Bills, bills, and more bills as usual. Nothing from Reggie. I'd sent him a couple of letters and emails, even text messages but had received no response. I was beginning to wonder if he'd even received them. I shrugged and then laid the mail down on the table.

After a long, relaxing bath and a dinner of leftover take-out Chinese food, I settled down on my sofa with a cup of hot tea and my notebook. I spent most of my evenings right there on that sofa writing music or letters to Reggie. This time, it was another letter.

*Dear Reggie,*

*I hope everything is going well with you in Italy. It feels good to be back in Dallas, back in my own home and my own space. Sure, there are more than a few bad memories here, but I've decided to make new memories, good memories.*

*I'm back in the studio with a new producer, "Pete the Beatmaker". Pete's great and we're creating some really good stuff. It's kind of a cross between Delta Blues and Neo Soul, real cutting edge stuff. I wrote the lyrics to all of the songs and most of them were inspired by you or our relationship. I'm going to send you a copy of the completed CD, and I hope you like it.*

*Well, I'm still sober. Four months now, and counting. I'm attending AA meetings at a church in my neighborhood and believe it or not, I've been going to church every Sunday, too. Quite a change for a former heathen, huh? Oh, but you always believed in me anyway, didn't you? You know, you were right about something else. God did take this mess of a life I was living and work a miracle. With the exception of missing you, I'm actually pretty content with my life. I know that I owe that to God and to you for loving me unconditionally.*

*I miss you, Reggie, and I know I've said it a thousand times, but I really am sorry. I wish a million times that I could go back in time and change what I did, but I can't. I wish I hadn't kept the truth from you, but I did. But more than that, I wish you'd forgive me.*

*Well, it's getting late and I've got to be back in the studio bright and early in the morning. I love you, Reggie. I still wear your ring, and I'll never take it off. I'll wait for you no matter how long it takes for us to be together.*

*Love,*

*Your Superstar, Bobbie*

I pulled the sheets of paper from the notebook and hugged them against my chest before folding them and slipping them into an envelope. I addressed the envelope to Reggie's home in Milan and then slipped it into my purse. I turned the light off and went to bed where, after saying my prayers, I soon drifted off to sleep.

♫♫♫

The next morning as I stood in the studio, headphones covering my ears, I tapped the mic and then nodded at Pete. The mellow, mid-tempo track began to play in my ears and I closed my eyes. The song we were recording was called "But You." I'd written it for Reggie. I tilted my head to the side, took a deep breath, and once the intro was finished, I began to sing the lyrics:

*"Once upon a time, a little girl was lost*
*She thought she had it all, but didn't realize the cost*
*But then one day she saw her life for what it really was*
*A mess, disaster, catastrophe and knew it was because*

*Real love had evaded her; it was nowhere to be found*

*In its place a miserable space, heartache abound*
*Her heart was broken, her dreams shattered*
*Gone was happiness, delight, and all that mattered*

*But you, oh baby, you stepped right in*
*Yes you, you made things right again*
*You were everything she needed to know*
*But baby, why did you have to go…"*

I sang the song from my heart and even if I do say so myself, I sounded *good*, real good. There's nothing like real-life, raw emotion to stir up a gift. For the first time, I felt like I'd made magic in the studio, and I can't even explain how that felt.

♫♫♫

"Ladies and gentlemen, The House of Blues presents the beautiful, the incomparable, Ms. Bobbie BluAnn Brooks!"

I held my place onstage as the curtains rose. Dressed to kill in tight brown leather pants, a gold tank top, and gold heels; my hair, now fashioned in shoulder-length dread locks, swung as I tapped my foot and nodded to the opening guitar riff of my newest single, "Turn Around". It was May and this was the opener to a short promotional tour I was embarking on to support my new CD. I was with my old band, complete with a new back-up singer, doing what I love, and I was having the time of my life.

"Hello, Dallas! Y'all glad to see your girl tonight?" I yelled into the mic.

The crowd roared enthusiastically in response.

I smiled and said, "Y'all looking good out there! You ready to groove with me?"

Another roaring response.

I smiled. "Well here we go! This is the first single off my new CD, *Lovely Blues*. It's called 'Turn Around'. I hope y'all like it."

I smiled again, took a deep breath, and began to sing the song that, like most of the other songs on *Lovely Blues*, I'd written for Reggie Darrough. Anyone in the audience could tell that I felt and meant every single word that I sang…

*"Woke up this morning*
*You weren't there*
*No kiss, no hug*
*No feelings to share*

*My heart is broken*
*My soul bruised blue*
*I miss you, baby*
*All I want is you*

> *I got plenty of money, my car is nice*
> *But to have you back, I'd give it all up twice*
>
> *I gotta turn this thing around*
> *It's my mission to get you back*
> *I love you baby, can't nothin' change that…"*

I closed my eyes and imagined that Reggie was sitting in the front row. I smiled and sang to him and only him and when I was finished, I was greeted with applause the likes of which I'd never heard before.

The show was a hit and afterwards, the audience gobbled up the copies of *Lovely Blues* that were for sale on site. I decided to skip the after party, opting instead to head straight home and into bed. Tomorrow was Houston, and I was definitely ready to put on another show.

I arrived home late that night and parked my truck in the driveway. I walked to my front door and nearly jumped out of my skin when I felt a hand on my shoulder. I spun around with my key sticking out from between my fingers, poised to jab whoever it was in the eye.

Standing before me was the shell of a man I once knew well. I felt like I was looking at a ghost.

"Junior?" I asked. "Is that you?"

"Yeah Bobbie Ann, it's me," he said barely above a whisper.

"What are you doing here so late? You scared me to death!" I nearly shouted.

He shrugged and said, "I wanted to see my baby sister."

"Junior, it's the middle of the night. I just did a show, and I'm really tired."

"Yeah, I know. I was gonna come to the show, but I didn't have money for a ticket."

"Well, If I'd known you were in town and wanted to come, I woulda gotten you some tickets. I'm doing Houston next."

"Yeah, well I wouldn't have no way of getting to Houston. Um, can I come in? Rest my bones for a minute. I been waiting out here for a while now."

I hesitated. Yes, he was my brother, but he was also a drug addict, and they weren't known for being very trustworthy. What if he tried to rob me? I said a quick, silent prayer for protection and then decided to let him in.

"Okay, well, come on in."

I unlocked the front door and led Junior to the kitchen where I offered him a seat at the table.

"This is a really nice place you got here, sis," Junior said as he eyed the room.

"Thanks," I said as I walked over to the counter and laid my purse down. "You want some coffee? I was gonna make myself some."

"Oh yeah. Thanks, that'll be great."

I inspected Junior as I scooped the coffee from the can. There in the bright light of the kitchen, I got a better view of him. His six foot frame was rail thin, and he was wearing a dingy t-shirt and dirty, tattered khaki pants. His sneakers looked worn and run-over. His thick hair was matted and his brown skin was ashen. There were bags under his eyes. I wondered when he had last eaten a good meal or taken a bath.

I finished loading the coffeemaker and then sat down across from Junior. "How've you been?" I asked.

"Okay."

"Well, you don't look okay. Mama's been really worried about you."

Junior laughed. "Since when did you and Mama start talking? The last thing I remember you saying was that you were gonna get out of her house and never turn back. Isn't that what you did?"

I dropped my eyes. "I've done and said a lot of things in the past, most of which I'm not proud of, Junior. I've learned better, and me and Mama get along pretty good now."

He rolled his eyes. "Good for you, sis."

"Come on, Junior. How are you, *really*?"

"What you want me to say, Bobbie Ann? You want me to confess to being a crackhead or something? Okay fine! I smoke crack! I love it! I'm having the time of my life being a drug addict. Woo hoo! It's a thrill a minute. I came over here tonight looking for a handout from you so that I can go buy and smoke some more! You satisfied now?" He said, raising his voice.

"Junior, I was just—"

He stood up from the table, knocking the chair over in the process. "Just what? What, Bobbie Ann? You were just judging me. That's what you were doing. You were sitting over there in your fine house, with all your money, and you were judging me. Well, you don't know what I been through. You have no idea why I'm like this!"

I shook my head. "No Junior, I don't have any room to judge anybody. I'm not perfect, and I'll be the first to admit it."

He scratched the back of his head and turned towards the door. "Forget it. This was a bad idea. I'mma just go now."

I stood up and walked over to him, blocking his exit. "Look Junior, just stay and have a cup of coffee. I'll make you a sandwich, too. Just talk to me for a little bit and then you can go. I won't stop you."

Junior looked at me and rubbed his stomach. "Yeah, well I *am* kinda hungry."

"Then stay. You're my brother, and I just wanna talk to you for a minute, okay? I missed you."

"Alright."

Junior picked up the chair and sat back down. I fixed him a couple of ham sandwiches and both of us cups of coffee. As Junior began to eat, I sat down at the table and resumed our conversation.

"How's Nora Lee?" I asked.

Junior shrugged and between bites of his sandwich said, "I don't know."

"Why don't you know?"

"She left me right after we came here to Dallas."

"Well, when did y'all get here?"

"A couple of months ago."

"And you haven't seen her since? Aren't you worried about her?"

"Naw, she said she was tired of living like this and was gonna get cleaned up. I figured she went to rehab and was living her life."

"Well, don't you wanna get cleaned up too, Junior?"

He looked up at me. "It ain't that easy, Bobbie. Don't you think I've *tried*? You think I wanna be like this? I can't do it. I can't kick the stuff."

"I know you can't do it by yourself. But you can with God's help."

Junior shook his head. "You've been talking to Mama. She's got you on that God stuff, too, huh?"

"Look Junior, God is the only one who can help you, and that's the truth. I know it is."

Junior waved his hands. "I don't wanna hear that crap! I grew up listening to and believing that stuff. I know better now! God don't care nothing about me."

"Look, I know what I'm talking about, Junior. I used to feel the same way."

"How? How Bobbie? What in your perfect life qualifies you to tell me what I need or how I feel?"

"Up until a few months ago, I was an alcoholic and I nearly drank myself to death. My husband even left me. I'm sober now but only with God's help.

Junior looked at me skeptically. "You making that up?"

"No, I'm not. It's the truth. Being in this business is hard on you and that, plus a lot of personal problems, led me to drink."

"But you still got your career and your home. You didn't lose everything. I lost everything, Bobbie Ann. *Everything.* I got no reason to get clean."

I reached across the table and grasped his hand. "I can think of at least two reasons, Junior. You have two beautiful, smart daughters who need a father."

Junior shook his head. "But Bobbie, you don't know what I've done. If I get clean I'll have to face it."

"Junior, I've done some bad stuff, myself and one thing I can tell you for sure is that carrying it around and beating yourself up about it won't help anything. You can tell me and I can guarantee you'll feel better getting it off your chest."

Junior sighed and dropped his eyes to the table. "When I was in college, I found out that Daddy wasn't my real father. My real father showed up at the college and told me. I called Mama and Daddy and they confirmed it and on top of that, I found out that the dude raped Mama, and that's how she got pregnant! It was like everything I knew to be true was a lie, and I couldn't handle it. That plus the pressure of keeping my scholarship was just too much for me so I dropped out and went home. I hooked up with Nora. She was already into smoking weed and one thing led to another. Before I knew it, we had two kids, and we were both strung out on the hard stuff.

"Mama and Daddy came to take the girls from us, and I'll never forget how Daddy looked at me and told me how disappointed he was in me. I looked at him and cussed him out. I told that I didn't care what he thought because he wasn't my father anyway. I told him that my real father was a piece of trash and that I was just like him. The look on his face told me that I had really hurt his feelings, but I didn't care. I didn't care about anyone but myself and that dope.

"That was the last time I talked to Daddy. He died a coupla years later. I never apologized. I should've, but I never did. Daddy was good to me. If my real father hadn't told me the truth, I never woulda figured it out, because Earl Brooks treated me like his own. Now, every time I close my eyes, I see Daddy's face and all the hurt I caused him. He died thinking that I hated him, and I hate myself for it. And after all that, my real father ain't never try to find me again. It was like he just came into my life long enough to tear everything up."

Junior buried his face in his hands and I stood up, walked over to him, and wrapped my arms around him. He laid his head on my chest and sobbed. I stood there and hugged him until his tears had dried.

"Junior, would you stay here tonight?" I asked.

He shook his head. "Naw, I can't."

I looked him in the eye. "Please stay. We can talk more in the morning, and if you decide that you're ready to get clean, I'll help you."

Junior hesitated and then said, "Okay."

It was already late, but I showed him to one of the spare bedrooms and then went to bed myself. When I woke up the next morning, Junior was gone.

# TWENTY-FOUR

### "Sky is Crying"

IT had been a week since I'd seen Junior, and as I lay asleep in my bed, the buzzing of my cell phone on the night table woke me up. It was the middle of the night. I flicked on the lamp and checked the caller ID. It was Mama, and it was 3:00 A.M. Why would she be calling so late? Then a feeling of panic flooded me. Had something happened to her or one of the girls?

I bolted up in the bed and answered the phone. "Hello?" I said, groggily.

"Bobbie Ann?" Mama asked. I guess I really didn't sound like myself, but then again, it *was* the middle of the night.

"Yes, ma'am. It's me. Is something wrong?"

"I just wanted you ta know dat Cassie passed away tonight."

"Oh no! Reggie's mom? Is Reggie there?"

"Yeah, he been here a coupla weeks now. He was wit' her when she passed."

"Oh, Lord. I know he must be hurt."

"He is. Bobbie, you should come be wit' him. He need you."

"Yes ma'am. Um, I have a show in Shreveport tomorrow. Afterwards, I'll head straight to Arkansas."

"Okay, I'll be looking for ya."

After I'd hung up, I said a prayer for Reggie and found it hard to get back to sleep.

♫♫♫

It was 8:00 A.M. I was sitting outside Reggie's mother's house in my truck, nervously staring at the front door. I'd left Shreveport right after my show and had made it to Willisville around 4:00 A.M. I'd spent the early morning hours lying wide awake in bed in my mother's house, trying to figure out what I'd say to Reggie and how I'd say it. I'd left my mom's house for Ms. Cassie's at 7:50 A.M., what I deemed was a respectable enough hour to visit.

I glanced over at Reggie's SUV which sat next to a shiny black Mercedes. I was pretty sure that it must have belonged to some family member, and although I didn't want to wake the entire house, I needed to see Reggie. I just wanted him to know that I was there for him.

After a little more nervous contemplation, I stepped out of my vehicle and onto the gravel driveway. I slowly made my way to the front door of the modest house and as I stepped onto the front porch, took a deep breath. I ran my fingers through my locs, smoothed the front of my white oxford shirt, and then knocked on the door. I stood and waited for a few minutes and had decided to leave when the door swung open to reveal a stunningly beautiful, dark-skinned woman. She was tall and thin with gorgeous bone structure, almond-shaped eyes, and full round lips. She wore her jet black hair in small individual braids.

"Yes?" She asked, raising her perfectly arched eyebrows.

"Um, is Reggie here?" I asked, looking past her into the house.

She smiled. "I'm sorry, he's asleep. Are you one of his cousins or a friend of his? I'm his wife, Caprice." She extended her hand.

If I had been eating or chewing gum, I surely would've choked. Wife? I thought they were divorced. Were they back together and married again? No wonder he hadn't responded to my letters or messages.

I blinked and then managed to reply with, "Um, well just tell him that Bobbie came by."

Without waiting for her reply or shaking her hand, I turned and walked briskly back to my truck. I was on the edge of crying, and I didn't want her to see me. I drove back to my mama's house, sobbing the entire way and once I'd parked in her driveway, I laid my head against the steering wheel and cried like a baby. I'd messed up. I'd really messed everything up and now there was no way we'd get back together. What was I going to do?

I closed my eyes and prayed and cried and before I knew it, Mama was standing next to my truck, knocking on my window.

I wiped my face and rolled my window down. "Yes ma'am?"

"Bobbie Ann, you alright out here?" Mama asked, with a look of concern on her face.

I shook my head. "Mama, I just don't know. I really don't."

Mama frowned. "What happened? You talk ta Reggie?"

"No, because his *wife* answered the door. I just left. I didn't know what else to do."

Mama raised her eyebrows. "Wife? Reggie ain't got no wife. I woulda heard about that."

"Well, the lovely Caprice says different."

"Caprice? Ain't they divorced?"

"She's at his mama's house answering the door like she's the lady of the manor. Obviously, they're back together. I thought the truth was supposed to make things right, but all it's done is mess everything up."

"Unh uh, he jus' hurt and confused. You go back over there right now!"

"And do what Mama?"

"Fight for him!"

I opened the truck door and slid out onto the driveway. I stood next to Mama and shook my head."It's too late for that. I had my chance, and I messed it up."

Mama put her hands on her hips and asked, "Then what you gone do Bobbie?"

I shrugged. "I'mma go to the funeral and pay my respects and then I'm going back to Dallas. My next show is in five days, Atlanta."

"Well, I pray he see what he doin'. He don't love no Caprice. He love you," she said as she pointed to me.

I shook my head. "Yeah, well, I thought so too."

♫♫♫

I hadn't been inside Willisville Baptist Church in months and as I looked around at the familiar faces surrounding me, I realized that I actually missed this little church and its congregation. I sat next to Mama in my black dress and looked across the aisle at Reggie who sat next to Caprice and three children whom I assumed were hers.

It was all I could do not to burst into tears. I felt pain for Reggie, knowing how dear his mother was to him. But I felt pain of my own because of what I'd lost in losing him. The more I thought about it, the more I knew that I loved him and the more it hurt. I dabbed my eyes with a tissue and saw that Mama was doing the same. I reached over and grabbed her hand and offered her a weak smile. Across the aisle, I could see that Reggie and Caprice were holding hands as well.

We sat through the long service, during which several of Ms. Cassie's friends spoke of her character and strength, and afterwards, drove to St. Peter's cemetery for the interment ceremony. I stood with Mama and cut my eyes away from Reggie, who sat next to the grave with Caprice by his side.

Once the interment was over, I reluctantly followed Mama over to Reggie and of course, Caprice, so that she could offer him her condolences. As she reached up and hugged him, I stood back and did my best to be unnoticed. But of course it didn't work. Caprice quickly outed me.

She looked at me and said, "Bobbie, right? Reg, this is the Bobbie that came by the other morning."

Reggie's head snapped up, and he stared at me with eyes full of sadness. He stared at me but did not say a word.

I was the one who broke the awkward silence. I looked up at him and said, "Um, I'm really sorry about your loss, Reggie. I'm praying for you."

He looked me in the eye for a moment and then simply said, "Thank you."

I turned to leave, fighting the urge to fall against his chest and wrap my arms around him. I loved him and the look I saw in his eyes when he saw me told me that he still loved me, too. As I climbed back into my truck and gripped the steering wheel, I twisted Reggie's ring around on my finger and thought to myself, *Just wait.* I smiled at Mama and then headed back to the church where dinner was to be served.

# TWENTY-FIVE

## "Ain't Understanding Mellow?"

*"DON'T forget me*

*Don't erase me from your mind*

*Don't lose our memories*

*Our special place in time*

*Remember our first touch*

*The way it made us feel*

*Think about those times*

*As vivid as a motion picture reel*

*Because the love we have is rare*

*My heart belongs to you*

*Your ring I still wear*

*My love for you is true…"*

On stage at the Orpheum Theater in Memphis, I sat on a stool in front of the sold-out crowd singing the lyrics to the second single from my *Lovely Blues* CD. It was a ballad and it was written for Reggie. Dressed in dark blue skinny jeans and a white off-the-shoulder sweater, it was all I could do not to cry as the words spilled from my lips. This was the final performance in a string of sold-out shows, and I was eager to get back to Dallas for a break.

I finished "Remember Me" and bowed in response to the audience's enthusiastic applause. Dressed in their summer's best, they had extended me the warmest of welcomes and had shown me nothing but love throughout the entire set.

As I disappeared backstage and headed into my dressing room, I smiled at the many gifts and flowers from well-wishers that crowded the small space. I sat down at the make-up mirror to begin the task of cleaning my face. No after-party for me. I planned to head straight to the hotel and then to the airport bright and early in the morning.

I'd barely been seated two minutes when I heard a knock at the door. Curious, I approached the door with a slight frown on my face.

"Yes? Who is it?" I asked through the door.

"It's Ray, Ms. Brooks. There's someone out here to see you." Ray was my new bodyguard. Since I traveled alone, I figured that I needed someone to protect me.

"Oh, uh, who is it?" I said, the door still shut between us.

"A Mr. Morgan," Ray answered.

My frown deepened. Clyde? What was he doing here? I thought about telling him to leave and then decided against it. I wasn't mad at Clyde anymore, so what the heck?

"Oh, okay," I said and then opened the door.

On the other side stood Clyde and behind him, out-sizing him by several inches in height and pounds in weight was Ray. I nodded at Ray and allowed Clyde to enter the room. Clyde looked nice in a black suit and tie. In his hands, he held a bouquet of pale pink roses which matched his dress shirt.

I smiled. "Clyde, what are you doing here?"

He shrugged. "Well, I was in town on business, and I heard you were performing here tonight, so I decided to catch your show."

"Oh, well, come on in and have a seat." I nodded toward the loveseat, feeling a little strange. I hadn't been alone in a room with Clyde in a long, long while.

"Um, these are for you," he said, extending the roses toward me.

"Well, thanks Clyde. They're beautiful." I took the flowers from him and sat in a chair next to the loveseat.

"That was one hell of a show, little girl. That new sound suits you real well," Clyde said as he sat down on the loveseat.

I smiled proudly. "Yeah, well I guess a million people agree with you. I got my first platinum plaque."

Clyde's eyes widened. "Really? That's great Bobbie!"

"Yeah, I feel pretty good about it. I poured my heart and soul into those songs."

"Yeah, I can tell. You know, I always said you'd go platinum one day. I knew you had it in you."

I smiled and nodded. "Yeah, you did." We sat there in awkward silence for a few moments and then I said, "Um, what kinda business you here for, if you don't mind my asking."

"Oh no, I don't mind. I gotta a new singer I'm managing. She's gotta show tonight."

I cleared my throat and said, "Sabrina?"

He shook his head. "No, her name's Phaea-Renee."

I raised my eyebrows. "Oh, okay. She any good?"

Clyde leaned forward. "Now come on, little girl. I managed you, and you're the best. Now, she ain't you, but you know if I'mma deal with her she's gotta be good."

"That's great, Clyde. Maybe I'll get a chance to hear her sometimes."

Clyde straightened up in his seat. "Hey, why don't you come to the show with me? It's at a little night spot across town."

I shook my head. "Oh, Clyde, I've gotta get dinner and get to bed. I've got an early flight in the morning."

"Aw, come on, little girl. You don't have to stay for the whole show. Just a few songs, and they serve food at the club. You get dinner and a show on me. Whattaya say?"

"Clyde, I don't know…"

"Look, dinner and a show, no strings attached, I promise."

I thought for a minute and then shrugged and said, "Okay, just let me freshen up first."

♫♫♫

We rode in Clyde's rented SUV to the small club across town where, once inside, we sat right in front of the stage at Clyde's "reserved" table and settled down for the show. We ordered dinner, a fried catfish plate for me and a barbecue pork sandwich for Clyde, and listened to the music as Phaea-Renee prepared to take the stage. While we waited, Clyde filled me in on how he'd met Phaea in Houston a few months earlier and was working on securing her a one album recording deal.

"Wow, Clyde. That's really great. But then again, you've always been a great manager. The best." I said.

"Just not that great a husband, huh?" he asked with a sheepish expression on his face.

I shrugged. "It was what is was, Clyde, and it's over now. I'm as much to blame for that as you are. It takes two people to make a relationship and to break it."

Clyde shook his head. "Yeah, well, like the old song says, if I could turn back the hands of time. I sure would treat you better, little girl. Ain't found another like you; never will."

I smiled. "I know exactly how you feel, Clyde."

Clyde leaned across the table and asked, "You happy, Bobbie? I mean really happy?"

I took a sip of my water and said, "As happy as I *can* be. I'm enjoying performing my new music and I've got tons more songs written. I'm *so* ready to get back in the studio."

Clyde smiled. "Well, I bet you'll crank out even more hits. You're gonna have a wall full of platinum plaques after awhile."

"Thanks, Clyde."

"Yeah," he said.

Our food arrived shortly thereafter and so did Phaea. We ate and watched as she performed a couple of songs she'd written. She *was* good. She was tall and lanky with smooth, dark chocolate skin and long legs. She wore her hair in cornrows and her red dress was skin tight. Her huge eyes were expressive as she sang with a style that was a cross between old-school soul and smooth jazz. After she'd finished her third song, a cover of an Anita Baker song, she exited the stage for a short break.

"Wow, she's great! Maybe she could open for me sometimes," I said.

"Bobbie, that would be great! I'd really appreciate it."

I nodded. "No problem. She'd be a good addition to my show. She's like a breath of fresh air."

I was looking around at the crowd and tapping my foot to the music provided by the DJ when Clyde startled me by asking, "You ever think that maybe we might get back together?"

I bucked my eyes. Had he just asked what it sounded like he'd asked? "Um, Clyde I don't really have those kind of feelings for you anymore. I feel like we can be good friends, though."

"Oh, okay." He paused and then added, "You got someone special in your life now?"

"Well, Clyde do you really think that's any of your business?"

He held up his hands. "Okay, I'm sorry. It's just that I see the ring, but where's the man?"

"Clyde—" I began, but he interrupted me.

"It's okay, I know it's not my business. I just hope he knows how lucky he is." He reached across the table for my hand and said, "You were the best thing that ever happened to me, and I threw you away for a woman who couldn't ever hold a candle to you. I really miss you. I'm sorry, Bobbie."

I sighed. "Clyde, I wasn't exactly 'wife of the year', and I know it. I was too needy and weak. Anyway, I forgave you a long time ago. You live and learn, right?"

He looked at me and said, "Yeah, but some lessons sure are hard-learned, little girl."

I nodded. "Who you tellin'?"

♫♫♫

It was a lovely August day and instead of playing outside, I'd decided to paint my bedroom ceiling. Ever since I was a little girl, I'd wanted a blue sky with fluffy white clouds on my bedroom ceiling and on this day, I'd decided to make my own wish come true. I was at the top of the ladder rolling away with jazz pouring from my stereo when I felt my cell phone vibrate in the hip pocket of my jeans. I pulled the vinyl glove off of my left hand and reached into my pocket.

Imagine my shock when I checked the screen of my phone and saw that it was Reggie's number. My heart began to race, and I nearly fell while trying to climb down the ladder. I juggled the roller in one hand while I pressed the button to accept the call with the other.

"H…hello?" I answered almost too eagerly. I hadn't spoken to Reggie since his mother's funeral back in the spring.

"Bobbie?" His voice nearly brought tears to my eyes. He sounded so good.

I sat down on the side of my bed and held my hand to my mouth for a moment and then said, "Yes. Reggie?"

"Yeah, how you been?"

I wanted to yell all kinds of crazy cliché movie-line type responses at him like, "I'm nothing without you" or "Without you, my life's been meaningless."

But instead, I replied with, "Okay, you?"

"I'm alright. I've been listening to that CD you sent me."

I blinked back tears and said, "Oh, you got it? I wasn't sure."

"Yeah, it's real nice, Bobbie. Different from your old stuff."

I smiled. "Yeah, it is, but people seem to like it."

"I bet they do. It sounds really good."

"Thank you, Reggie."

"Bobbie Ann, I called because I needed to ask you a question."

I looked down and saw that the roller had dripped a puddle onto the plastic tarp that covered the rug. I set it in the pan and then said, "Okay."

"You remember in one of your letters you said that you still wear my ring?"

I glanced at my hand. "Yeah, I'm wearing it right now."

"And that you'd wait for me, no matter how long?"

I nodded as if he could see me through the phone. "Yeah."

"Did you mean it?"

"Of course I did, Reggie. I love you. Why?" I asked. Before he could answer, I heard my doorbell ring. *Dear Lord, who is that at a time like this*? I wondered.

"Is that your doorbell?" Reggie asked.

"Yeah, but it can wait," I said.

"No, go ahead and get it. I'll hold on."

I sighed in disgust and strode down the stairs to the front door with my cell phone in my hand. I hoped that I'd run whoever it was away quickly with my horrible appearance. I was wearing an old scarf on my head, worn white shorts and a paint-splattered white t-shirt.

"Who is it?" I asked through the door, my hand on the chain.

"Delivery," answered the voice on the other side.

Now I was really getting annoyed. I wasn't expecting any delivery and whoever this guy was really needed to go away. I unlocked the door and then swung it open with a frown on my face and saw the most beautiful sight I'd ever seen standing before me. Reggie was on the other side of the door holding his phone to his ear and smiling brightly.

I felt my eyes fill with tears as I asked, "W…what are you doing here?"

Reggie lowered the phone and looked me in the eye. "Well, I've been here, in town, for a few days now, wanting to see you."

"Reggie, I—" I began to speak, but was overtaken by the emotions filling me as I looked upon the face of the only man I'd ever truly loved.

Reggie wiped my tears away with his fingertips as they spilled from my eyes onto my cheeks. "I came here to reclaim something I lost. Something that once belonged to me," he said.

I looked up at him and into his eyes. "What? What did you lose?"

He cupped my face in his hands and smiled. "The love of my life in the form of a pretty little girl from Arkansas. A girl I've loved since I was a boy."

I sniffled. "You never lost her. She's been right here waiting for you. Praying that you'd come back to her."

Reggie leaned over and planted a long kiss on my lips, and I think I might have dropped my phone in the process.

"So, you forgive me?" I asked once our lips had parted.

"Only if you forgive me."

Confused, I asked, "For what?"

"For deserting you and leaving you to make that decision on your own." He pulled me into his arms, and I laid my head against his chest.

"I missed you so much, Reggie," I said.

"I'll never leave you again. I promise."

I looked up at him. "What about Caprice?"

"What about her?"

"Back at your mom's house, she said she was your wife. I thought that you two were back together."

Reggie stepped back and looked me in the eye. "No, she *wanted* us to get back together, but that wasn't happening. She helped me through a tough time, and I appreciate her for it, but I never stopped loving you, and I never will."

I smiled. "I love you, Reggie."

He returned my smile and then said, "No more than I love you, Superstar."

# EPILOGUE

*I sat on the toilet, staring at the dipstick as if willing the little plus sign to form in the window. I could hear Reggie pacing outside the door. This had almost become a monthly ritual for us since we'd married. We spent plenty of time working on a baby only to see a minus sign in that window time and time again. Reggie wanted a baby. I wanted a baby. We'd prayed and prayed, been to the doctor time and time again. Still no baby. Scar tissue from the abortion was the problem. It wouldn't be impossible for me to get pregnant but it would be highly improbable. Improbable, that's what the doctor said.*

*I read the caption on the box. "Results in the blink of an eye." That was a lie. It felt like I'd been sitting there waiting for hours.*

*"Baby, you okay in there?" Reggie asked through the door.*

*"Yeah. You wanna come in?" I knew the answer. He was too nervous.*

*"Naw, I'm okay. Just let me know what it says."*

*"Okay."*

*I checked my watch. One minute left. I sighed. Please God. Please let it be positive. I closed my eyes and when I opened them, it was time. I couldn't look. I'd been disappointed so many times. I just couldn't look at it.*

*"Baby, can you come in here?" I said.*

*"What does it say?"*

*"I can't look this time. I need you to do it."*

*Silence from the other side of the door. He didn't want to do it. I knew he didn't, but I needed him to do it. More silence and then the bathroom door slowly creaked open. Reggie stood before me with a nervous look on his face.*

*I pointed to the dipstick. "It's right there."*

*He nodded and then picked it up. He stared at it for a long while and when he finally looked up at me, there were tears in his eyes.*

*"What does it say?" I asked.*

*He handed it to me. I looked at the result window and tears flooded my own eyes…*

For information about Alcoholics Anonymous, go to:

**http://www.aa.org/**

For abortion recovery information and resources, go
to:

**www.ramahinternational.org/**

For information about the author, go to

**http://adriennethompsonwrites.webs.com/**

www.ingramcontent.com/pod-product-compliance
Lightning Source LLC
Chambersburg PA
CBHW061139170626
46809CB00003B/916